THE LAST FLORIDIAN

Pete Clements

Black Rose Writing | Texas

The author grants the final approval for this literary material.

First printing

This is a work of fiction. Names, characters, businesses, places, events, and incidents are either the products of the author's imagination or used in a fictitious manner. Any resemblance to actual persons, living or dead, or actual events is purely coincidental.

ISBN: 978-1-68513-373-3
PUBLISHED BY BLACK ROSE WRITING
www.blackrosewriting.com

Printed in the United States of America
Suggested Retail Price (SRP) $19.95

The Last Floridian is printed in Bookman Old Style

*As a planet-friendly publisher, Black Rose Writing does its best to eliminate unnecessary waste to reduce paper usage and energy costs, while never compromising the reading experience. As a result, the final word count vs. page count may not meet common expectations.

Dedication

I am indebted beyond bounds to Dr Bonnie MacDougall Ph.D, published novelist and author of "Something Terrible About Love" and "Love, Ruthie."

THE
LAST
FLORIDIAN

CHAPTER ONE

Today will be different. I'm 25 this day and graduated University of Florida in Agricultural Administration, the first in my family to graduate college. I'm Clayton Ian McIver. I say prayers. Some my age don't. I do chores, listen to my folks, and respect them.

I was back home for my birthday. I've had my own place since college, but not for much longer, I suspect. We're celebrating together just the three of us in our family's two-story, white-frame Cracker house, out on the wrap-around covered porch—Mom, Dad and me. Mom usually bakes a cake, and we have lots of friends over, but not this time.

Since I was about twelve or fourteen, I worked in my daddy's business. It's existed for as long as I can remember. The citrus grove service business takes care of other people's groves from start to harvest. We hoped I'd take it over when Dad decided to retire. I hoped to apply what my college education provided to the business, 21st century farming technological advancements, increased production, quality, and profit.

Mama cut us each a slice of my birthday cake. Dad's head was low, and his voice was almost a whisper. He said, "Head south, Son. Take the kayak and head south. It's at all-stop hereabouts for the foreseeable future." This was his answer to his worries about me and my future. He felt that way for a long time.

It almost seems there's no stopping what's being described as the greatest threat in history to Florida agriculture and its farmers, the Greening Disease. It's bacteria spread by the insect, Asian citrus psyllid, and it infected 95% of our state's trees. There is no cure yet.

I don't think I've fully realized what's happening in Florida, the significance of Florida's natural look, oceans of whispering grass, swamps and wetlands, and endless pine forests. Every single aspect of this environment is interconnected, the economy and swamplands, land use and green space, population growth and farming, natural resources and clean water. It's like knitting. Drop a stitch, and it comes unraveled.

Everything is disintegrating. Agriculture, tourism, and the very stuff that runs the Florida economy are in a state of malfunction with the citrus belt on its knees.

I know what's right before my eyes. Just across from the mouth of Ocklawaha, where it meets the St. Johns, is a new, sprawling development. Hundreds of little, look-a-like, three-bedroom bungalows are thrown up where just yesterday, egrets, osprey, and hawks safely lived, bred, and flew free.

It's time for me to step into my own life here in Florida. It's a time unlike my parents' day and my childhood. It's time for me to take charge of me and learn to cope with change.

The day had finally come. Dad was right. There were little, if any, real jobs with a future. Dad's suggestion made sense to travel by kayak on the St. Johns River. He thought out the reasoning behind his suggestion to take the St. Johns south. I would be conveniently and inexpensively near centers of economic activity, some exclusive of agriculture, specifically citrus. There could be the possibility of real careers. Also, the roads and bus terminals are choked with hitchhikers, thieves, druggies and crazies. These days, as many as two thousand a day are coming into the state. Mom, at the last minute, begged me to take her egg money, take the bus, anything but kayaking the long river in the dark. Dad was right. Roads are more dangerous than any course through the swampland.

He reminded me, "Son, there was a time, before the railroads, when there were no roads. The St. Johns River was the main thoroughfare through the state. Paddlewheel steamboats from Jacksonville by the dozens went up and down most of its length."

He suggested, "Cling to the shallows on the eastern shore of Little Lake George, out of the river currents. Keep the rifle and pistol loaded and handy. Everything you've been taught on our hunting-fishing trips, Son. Beach for the night and hide the kayak best you can. Camp away from it, and kill campfire smoke when you bed down. In the dark, you'll be motionless. The predator won't see you, but you'll know he's there. You'll sense his movement. Mangrove branches, palm fronds will whip, rattle, change their sway. Night sounds and river smells will lose their rhythm, come and go, replaced anew and strange. Note the difference. Listen for the splash of sloshing boots. A twig will crackle and snap. The grass will swish and hiss. You'll smell him, tobacco, alcohol, that human odor of sweat. The slightest intensity and echo in the signals will suggest more than one. Sleep with the pistol in your crotch. You know the land. You've handled this water a hundred times. You're my son. You'll be fine...." I heard the catch in his throat, as he tried to end his sentence; barely able to whisper, "My Florida boy." Then came a try at that smile.

"Thanks." Thanks hardly seemed enough.

Dad, his eyes cast down at first, looked up at me, patted Mom's hand, and, for the first time in months, there was that smile again. I don't think he was trying to show confidence just for Mom; I think he saw himself in me. He felt pride, and it gave him hope.

Mom clung to him as they watched me pack. She put a hand up to her mouth as she held back tears. She whispered, "This day marks who Clayton Ian McIver will become."

CHAPTER TWO

Dawn marked a new day. I was on my way. Out beyond the point, my muddy Ocklawaha River oozed into the great and ancient river, the St. Johns. A layer of ocher fog hovered just above the water's surface. I blindly inched one foot ahead of the other, trying to sense the soft, muddy bottom, typical of shallows here in Florida's inland waters. The light chop sloshed over my knees.

In these mist-gray remnants of predawn, I walked blindly, sliding forward one foot at a time. The bottom gradually felt more firm, finally solid underfoot. I pushed the kayak out ahead of me, and the water crept up to my thighs, turning less murky-warm and more chilly with every step.

There was enough water, so I brought the kayak up against my right hip. Empty, it weighed scarcely a hundred pounds. It was loaded with gear, food, water, personal stuff, bow to stern and gunwale to gunwale.

The folks will undoubtedly want to hear every single detail about the trip. How would I remember it all? I heard myself laugh out loud, because Mom always complained that I left the good stuff out when I told her about my day. My laughing out loud made me think, *Heck, I can talk out loud. There's nobody to hear me for miles around. That will help me remember all the details when I'm telling people at home.*

I swung my right leg over the port gunwale, my foot placed exactly fore and aft on the boat-bottom's centerline, just forward of my stern seat and aft of the stern thwart. I gripped the gunwales. I brought my left leg aboard. A local Timucuan chief, long ago, watching my father capsize, showed him how, and he showed me.

I was on my way.

I headed south, which was, oddly, upstream. The St. Johns there snakes through the middle of what's called Little Lake George. In my teens, Dad, in this same kayak, dropped me off way up here, then headed south and finally, before dark, rode the stronger river currents back north to pick me up. He had duck or game, or both, aboard, or bass taken on a fly rod at sunset using his own tied artificial flies. I marveled at how they looked exactly like real flies that hatch from larvae, as the sun sank every evening. The low sun's angle sent a glassy shimmer over the water surface, the new hatch swarming just above it.

Just like I started to talk out loud to myself, the river water had its way of talking. I stuck my hand down in it, felt it, and checked the smell. The St. Johns has its own smells. They signal to a trained nose, send a message, what's decaying, what's shallow, what's clear, the clear often natural springs. There are dozens of natural springs and underground rivers, deep, clean, some fresh, some salty. They gush up through the limestone with headwaters, some hundreds of miles down from under the bottom of the ocean. The perfume of the floating vegetation and islands of hyacinths signaled the safest channels. One simply has to join the living natural realm there, seek with caution, find the way, learn to tell the real channel from the dead end creek where the grass, with inviting openings, stands ten feet above the water surface. I was leery of those and feared all the backtracking.

It's starting to get light. A blistering edge of sun oozes up in the east, soon to be bearing down like a torch. Surrounding floating hyacinth colonies, the saw grass, scrub and sable palm trees are getting a grayish pea green color. The water, a shimmering reflective foil, is a sight to behold.

I was comfortable in a rhythm. The miles slipped by, and morning turned into afternoon. Paddling seemed effortless. The feathering of the returning paddle blade—not raising it up clear after each stroke—made the going easy. There were two hundred-plus miles out ahead. Port paddle in, stroke, feather… starboard paddle in, stroke, feather. I was confident. I wouldn't fail.

This first section of the St. Johns, paddling south from Welaka on half-mile-wide, so-called Little Lake George, was familiar territory to me, although I never actually studied it before. On hunting and fishing trips, I was busy getting my gear ready, mounting reel to rod or shells to shotgun chamber, about to be dropped off. It was a matter of one paddle blade after another. The feathering certainly made it easier; I was grateful to have been taught correctly.

I tacked back and forth, southeast, then southwest, over that part of the river's endless oxbows. The ancient meanderings of water for 10,000 years couldn't decide as to a proper course north, but eventually, upstream, its headwaters became the mouth of the real Lake George. It's about 15 miles south. At my estimated average 2.0 knots, I'd be well into the afternoon. I realized I've been talking aloud, talking to no one, but that was OK. I was alone out here where the birds sometimes talk to themselves. I was just being like a bird and chirped my story out over the small waves I made.

I paddled way past noon, sweating under the afternoon sun.

Soon enough it was time to start looking ahead for my first campsite. I've never stayed the night out here. I'd keep an eye out, as I paddled, look for a patch of high ground, an old Indian midden or shell mound, dry, elevated, maybe an abandoned campsite shaded under a stand of pines. Even if I passed one early, before dusk, I could always double back. I've never set up a campsite either. Alone, it was a new deal.

CHAPTER THREE

Finally, nearing the headwaters of Little Lake George, passing steep, sandy banks and dense, tall, pine forest, close to the mouth of huge, open Lake George, I saw smoke in the distance curling up out of the trees. It could have been a cloud, but it rose uninterrupted, straight up, as if from a sheltered chimney. It couldn't be more than half a mile away. I didn't see beached ski boats yet or hidden canoes or clusters of airboats. That smoke must mean people. We would soon see.

I paddled ten minutes to get close.

It wasn't a cloud. It was definitely smoke.

A grassy point extended out about fifty feet on the east shore. Grass stood tall in maybe two to four feet of tannic-colored water, stained by dead vegetation on the bottom. The wall of grass blocked any view beyond.

I paddled, quickly but quietly, barely breaking water, then stopped and listened. Only mosquitoes buzzed up close.

I rounded the point and slid through grass and shallows up onto the soft shore. The kayak's bow scraped over the nearly white sand of crushed shell and tiny limestone grains, scattered dead, brown leaves, and hip-high grass beyond.

Beached, I stepped out and started up a well-worn path. It was ground-up snail shells and soil made of dead vegetation, scattered cabbage scrub. A yellow canoe was dragged next to the path.

A hundred yards ahead, a couple sat on the ground around the smoking embers of last night's campfire. The whitish-gray wispy column reached up through the trees.

I stepped forward, not trying to hide my footsteps over the crackling leaves and twigs.

"Hello," I said. Their backs to me, a boy and girl, maybe my age, mid-twenties at most, sat in the clearing and leaned against the trunk of a pine tree. There was no answer. Maybe they didn't hear me. Closer, I said it again. They didn't answer. I slowly reached to put my right hand on my hip holster; it wasn't there, of course. I was not armed, but hell, it was broad daylight. It was strange. They just sat there as if talking to one another. From my angle, she appeared quite pretty, reddish dark brown hair to her shoulders, long, tanned legs, and cutoffs. He was of a different cut—unkempt long, dark hair, untrimmed shaggy beard, wrinkled dark T-shirt, and shoeless.

They surely could hear my approaching footsteps crunching on the dry ground. They both sat strangely, rod-stiff backs, staring straight ahead at one another, as if in shock.

"Morning, Folks." I tried to cheerfully announce myself. *Are they meditating? Am I intruding on some midday ritual?*

I was standing right next to them. I've never seen anything like it. It's common among the young, this new distant social stance, not arguing, just ignoring, distrusting, excluding all but our own generation. There's the whole drug scene, here, everywhere, all over, but....

The sight chilled me.

I forced my gaze upward and away, scrolling without seeing the trees to figure out if what I may have seen is true. Was the reality I sensed or saw for a split second really reality? Finally, unavoidably, I looked down again and stared at the syringes sticking out of both of them. They were dead.

My head swam, and I was just like stone, but I couldn't just stand there. I ran for the kayak to grab my cell phone. I prayed for cell service out there. I hit 9-1-1 and waited. The silence of the area and the picture screamed at me like a whole wild orchestra, every instrument tuning separately, each trying to be heard all at once. Every panther, screeching hawk, bear, hissing snake, and gator out there was upon me.

Finally, after waiting for hours in the growing darkness, sitting in the kayak, the faint throbbing sound of the approaching helicopter grew louder. It would be the Putnam County Sheriff, probably deputies, detectives, and medical examiner people.

They questioned me, moved the bagged bodies to the 'chopper, gathered evidence, and finally left. The whoosh-whoosh-whoosh of the blades drifted away. All the while, I was somehow not present, and the time of their presence seemed a millisecond.

I returned, relieved, to the silence of the St. Johns. I sat in the kayak still stunned. Finally, I think I faintly detected the sound of a faraway nesting hen high in a tree calling her mate to hurry home. I shook my head to clear it and tried to hear what was so distant. It was almost indecipherable, but then it seemed louder, like a sound wave brought it to me, and it was a song, clear, throaty, hollow, and distant.

CHAPTER FOUR

The sheriff's people, the body bags, and the 'chopper were long gone.

I went to bed last night in the cockpit of the kayak. Dog tired in body and mind, I wrapped my jacket around me and pulled my hat down low over my eyes. Loneliness overwhelmed me.

That girl yesterday had a needle in her arm. I heard the medical examiner say it was a recreational drug laced with fentanyl. She wasn't any older than me. She was pretty and probably just going along with that guy she thought she loved. She'd hardly started living really.

I can't understand why so many of us cash out like the future is a concrete wall. I'll never forget that scene. Couldn't it have been different? Couldn't we have been cooking over that fire, the girl offering me a beer, she and I singing songs?

This was all the wrong mood. I had 200-plus miles ahead of me. Better let all that go and get back on track. I have to set a southerly course on big Lake George, the biggest in Florida after Okeechobee. I had no time to linger on that tragic scene.

Checking both GPS and chart, I saw the lake measures about eight miles wide and over twelve miles long. It meant over four hours south to the headwaters if I could shake the image of that dead girl and keep focused. The chart showed an old Air Force Bombing Range, abandoned, a mile wide and the full length of the lake. I'd stay half mile off Lake George's eastern shore. The chart showed water depth about four to eight feet, with no current.

I slipped down not far offshore. The depth on the chart matched the depth I saw peering over the side, five-six feet. Past the sun's reflection on the surface, I saw bottom, swaying grass, and several fish darting. Undulating on the surface, all I saw was a wavy outline of that girl's face. I couldn't shake it, then it was gone. I blinked.

The water surface turned grayish, misty. Looking up, I saw the sky starting to cloud over.

I looked south through the binoculars.

I should have known. Venturing alone, I should have stopped, looked, analyzed: it's a huge, shallow lake, no more than eleven feet deep. I couldn't see land west or south. It's low country with not a breath of air.

For the moment, most likely like most mornings, Lake George could fool. It was a flat mirror. The horizon was a shimmering line, vibrating with heat waves, and above that a white-hot band. Overhead, a perfect Florida blue, but Florida weather can change fast, jump up and bite you.

The signals were right in front of me.

South southwest was a big, anvil-shaped cumulus nimbus. Its top refused to explode and let the pent-up water evaporate upward. It spelled rain.

I let the binocs drop to my chest and stared.

I looked at a mammoth thunderhead of a storm, thunder and lightning, wind that would turn this flat lake with its shallow water into a nasty sea. I smelled the ozone. Wherever there's ozone, there's lightning.

Prepping for this venture, I learned an oddity: the St. Johns River channel is almost stagnant, as it claws through this big Lake George. Conservationists cheer when a storm hits, churning up the water; it brings oxygen to the sea life. I sat there alone in the kayak with no real stability. Freeboard was above the waterline six inches. It was obvious. Capsizing was practically inevitable.

Lesson #1, you can't panic in a kayak. You chill out, stay cool. *I've got to stay calm.* Like I was yesterday, waiting for the 'chopper. Maybe it was more like in shock, not really calm, but all my senses turned on. I felt and heard everything around me. The wind brushed my face, and a far-off distant heron calling her mate was like human sound like a song. It was a song, though far away, but it seemed just for me. I wish that girl from yesterday was alive.

Hey, this ain't it, Chief. Get over it. Stay focused. The real McCoy is bearing down, right at us.

I kept heading straight at the storm's east edge. I paddled hard. I could easily capsize, rolling several times, but the storm would never catch me. When two compass bearings don't cross, they can't collide.

I watched that monster's counterclockwise movement. The wind was from the east. First, the trick is to turn into it, avoid a broach. Timing every wave was key. One rogue wave can throw the bow off. *My reaction will be everything. I've got to paddle hard. My eyes must be frozen on every crest whipped by the wind.*

I was glad I was in a kayak, not a canoe.

If I was canoeing, I'd soon be swimming, fighting my life jacket, and out of control in dangerous waters. Kayaking, if I capsized, I'd be protected. I could right it with me safely aboard. I practiced it hundreds of times, the 360-degree Eskimo Roll, the slick maneuver to get me and the boat back upright.

Lightning flashed in the distance, blinding me for a second. The wind was up and slapping my face. It was wet. I got that faint taste of chlorine, ozone.

Now came the rain, nearly horizontal, stinging. This was the kind of day people die. It was like I was in a car, speeding, headlights like shafts piercing the black, but too late, the gray wall was dead ahead.

The wind quit hitting me on the ear. It hit me in the face. It was a wind shift. The storm was distant but right next to me. Wind backed from east through south to southwest. My heading was still east, so I was suddenly broadside. Waves were confused like water jostled in a bucket.

My boat's starboard bow rose up on a wave crest. The same happened astern, but there was no water under the center. I was in a valley. Momentum got me.

I was going over.

Paralleling the paddle to the downside rail as I capsized, I gulped air and held my breath.

I was upside down. My eyes were open, vision cloudy. Wind was gone in this new world. All was silent. Tiny bubbles escaped my mouth. Hanging down, I glimpsed the churning lake bottom.

I swung the paddle out 90 degrees. The blade feathered upward to get it close to the surface for leverage. My eyes followed the blade.

I hiked my right knee up fast, whipped my hips hard left to right to roll the hull, and with my outstretched arm, pushed the paddle blade down against the water.

I was upright.

The water raked off my face. I blinked it out of my eyes and got my bearings. I steadied and balanced just in case it all repeated.

I was closer to shore, washed in on cresting chop over the shallows. I saw the eastern shore and beach... high ground... well, high enough.

I would set up my tent, build a fire, cook up something special, dry my clothes, have a beer, and watch the stars.

CHAPTER FIVE

The voice, clear and throaty, hollow and distant, drifted low across the hot afternoon rural Florida-blue sky. As if the cirrus clouds could sing, the amplified sound threaded out over the faded, blue-and-white canvas-covered patio and blue umbrella tables everywhere. It floated west past the old, adjacent wooden, bulkheaded docks and out over the lapping, fast-moving St. Johns River.

The manager of the place immediately turned on the huge, multiple patio speakers and cranked up the volume. He knew a real drawing card when he heard one.

Out on the river, the slowly circling, ever-present fleet of divers, ski boats, fishing rigs, and airboats awaited the gathering of this Friday night's throng and the start of an always ruckus weekend. The boaters killed their motors as soon as they heard the incipient tones of song adrift, and their shouts and beer chants died in an instant. They simply listened to the cool until the song finally faded, as it mingled with the abutments of the four-lane road bridge that crossed the river. The bridge lifted Florida's State Road 520, Cocoa Beach to Orlando, up over the famous river.

One after another, a line of black Harley bikes dropped down off 520, lined up, and parked side-by-side out front to wait for the doors to open.

Passing motorists on 520, approaching the bridge, saw the big sign nobody could miss, next to the rise. It stood 40 feet high on a single concrete pole and announced the name. It's the hottest boater, biker, diver, airboat joint anywhere in the swamplands of East Central Florida. The sign read, *The Lone Cabbage, A Restaurant, Bar & Fish Camp.* That night, there would be hundreds, hundreds all weekend, and live music nightly 'til closing, right on up through the big Sunday-night fish fry.

The owners, following a game-changing and most-remarkable audition of a new talent, decided to make an unusual and unlikely decision. For their first time they offered   a   complete   change   in   the entertainment. They furloughed both the usual Country Western and Hard Rock bands for up to two weeks. They would lead the way and be the first to present the newest sound sensation to outgrow the South Carolina hills. The new Sound Of The South was Miss Joleen Rebecca Jackson.

***

Late afternoon, in the great old dining hall, on a small bandstand under the low, stained cypress ceilings, she rehearsed a cappella. A tiny ceiling-mounted key light sent a thin shaft of bright white down, catching her upturned face and cheekbones. Her shoulder-length auburn hair, streaked in silver, touched her shoulders. She wore a long-sleeved black T-shirt and shiny black skinny jeans. Microphone in hand, she stood alone in the dark.

It was her own rendition of the famous Country Rock star Florida native, Jake Owen's hit, *"Don't think He Can't Love You."* There wasn't another sound, just her a cappella:

"I learned the hard way, really learned really hard, that money don't grow on the trees.

There's a few things even big dog can't buy, the best things in life they call free.

So, girl, he can't buy you a big diamond ring, no house on the hill full a' life's finer things.

I'll tell you right now there's a whole lot a boy cannot do, but, Baby,... don't think he can't love you."

She let her arm with the mic drop down to her side and turned her neck slowly to release the mood, then abruptly startled and amused, she smiled. Across the room from her, behind the darkened bar in shadow, the manager stood applauding.

***

At around ten o'clock in the evening in the great dining hall, throughout the room, the clatter of silverware and tinkling glass was everywhere. Every table was full, some having turned twice, even three times. Waiters still scurried. The crowd was two deep at the bar. Every stool was occupied. Four bartenders mixed and poured, not the standard cold glass of dollar draft beer, but cocktails.

Joleen took a break between sets. She was up on the small bandstand with her trio in white boot-cut Levis, red thong sandals, and a sequined-sparkling black, long-sleeved tee.

"Once again, good evening, everybody. Thanks for that special Lone Cabbage reception here on your beloved St. Johns. It's good to be in Paradise." She perched casually on a bar stool, mic in hand, out front of the trio.

The Lone Cabbage manager watched.

A waiter, with what looked like a guest's request, approached the bandstand. Joleen looked down, smiled at him and listened. The waiter whispered to her, pointed at the front door, then, like a dart, ducked away and was gone.

She was shocked and stunned.

She looked up, her eyes darting all over the room, searching.

Silence fell on the front tables.

She jumped down off the bandstand and took long, hurried steps trying not to run. As she passed the tables, her wild eyes jumped to the faces of patrons as she quickly passed by.

The stunned manager didn't know what to think, as she rushed past.

She opened the front door, rushed out, and was gone. The door whooshed closed behind her.

The manager stood there staring at the door. The crowd, nervous and wondering what on earth, started to rise. A buzz rose as they checked with one another about what was going on. The manager turned to the crowd, hands up, palms up, gesturing as if it could all be just nothing, and then he lamely, pointlessly, tried to quiet the throng. Suddenly, shaking his head, he whirled and headed out the front door.

Standing outside in the dark, he saw nothing and no one.

It had only been a minute, yet there was nothing. He heard the pulsating un-muffled propeller roar of an airboat, throttle down. The sound headed south, slowly dissipating, as the sultry darkness closed in over the river.

CHAPTER SIX

The jet-black airboat on a steamy night on this Upper St. Johns River screamed southbound at a dangerous 30 to 40 miles-per-hour. It had been pedal-to-the-metal since leaving The Lone Cabbage. There were no headlights, running lights, or orange flag on a tall pole.

The helmsman carried no certificate of airboat operator training, as required by Florida law as of 2019. A directional controlling joystick was off his left hip. The automatic rifle, with its multi-round magazine, hung down on his right. Both he and his one passenger, elevated on a padded bench seat next to him, were without lifejackets and seatbelts. Hanging down uselessly from the sides of the seats, they flopped in the wind.

All up and down the river, wildlife, snakes, gators, insects, and wading birds chose, with the sun down, to move about, feed, and mate. Hidden fishermen sat quietly in small boats at anchor and waited for fish lines to go taut. Ski boats, full of chatter, bobbed within the walls of grass. Adventurous kayakers, canoeists, and lovers paused to rest and observe the quiet tropical night. The speed of an airboat, limited forward visibility, the darkness, and tall grass could end any of these lives that night.

This whole south section of the St. Johns had the look of ancient waters; it is said to be where it all began, as the prehistoric seas receded. Countless wild, tannic acid-stained streams meandered. Oxbows twisted in dead-end countering directions. Huge hundred-square-mile swaths of tall, dense, wispy, rustling, stinging swamp grass extended down through Orange, Osceola, and Brevard Counties. The actual navigable St. Johns River Channel was mostly indiscernible.

Joleen Rebecca Jackson, her ankle shackled to the leg of the elevated bench seat on starboard, sat next to the driver aboard the airboat. Still wearing her light sequined top and white Levi boot cuts, she was sopping wet from slamming into the wet night wind. Her body was wrapped in a filthy, old, yellow oilskin. Her face, red and strained, was hit by gnats and mosquitoes and pelted by stinging spray and the sharp-edged whipping strands of tall grass.

Over wind and engine roar, she shouted, "OK, Ricky... OK... you win. OK? I'll do whatever you say. But stop, Ricky. At least, slowdown."

She tried logic. "We're flying blind; we'll hit something unseen ... or someone. You'll kill us... and them. And then what's the point of all this?"

His head slowly swiveled until he was in her face, demanding, "Joleen! Tell me you love me. Say it. Say it."

"Ricky. Ricky, listen. You only think you love me. Please slow down now. Please. And please get me off this God-awful boat."

He put his hand on the throttle and eased it back. The prop feathered. The airboat slumped down in the water to a crawl.

Joleen could scarcely recall when all this first started. It was even before she left her home, where she was born, Anderson, South Carolina, to launch a singing career. He appeared one night where she was singing at a little club in the hip, newly rejuvenated West End District in popular Greenville. They talked.

He said he was on vacation, looking for a new spot to live. He seemed nice. He could be attractive and had "III" after his name. They went on a couple dates, but then, in ten days, maybe two weeks, he got clingy and possessive. He talked girlfriend-boyfriend, called early morning and late at night, and texted while she was working a gig in the evening.

She drew back. She had a career to chase.

Then it really started, the haunting and relentless stalking. He was like a child used to getting his way with his sulking. When she finally rejected his ultimatums and told him she was moving, leaving Anderson, he just stared at her. She read desperation in his eyes.

Richard Randolph Wentworth III, the son of the R. R. Wentworth's, was, along with his parents, a permanent gated community resident of Florida's ultra-exclusive Jupiter Island. He tracked Joleen from South Carolina, first to Jacksonville, then Orlando and Cocoa Beach.

When the Lone Cabbage management launched its promo in local newspapers, radio spots, plus online in targeted social media and boldly on their huge roadside sign, reading,

NOW, THE SILKY SENSATIONAL

MISS JOLEEN REBECCA JACKON

THE NEW SOUND OF THE SOUTH, he had her.

With everything uncomfortably quiet, she said, "Let me off somewhere near Melbourne, will you? I'll make a call, try to call off the dogs."

Ricky's head sunk to his chest. One hand drifted up to his forehead, rubbing slowly as if in thought, then dropped to cover his open mouth. He said nothing. He seemed lost.

Joleen sensed he might just listen. "The Lone Cabbage people spent a bundle on promoting my gig. They won't be happy with you, Ricky, threatening me with that message to the waiter. Good grief, Ricky, you'd open fire on a packed dining room if I didn't come with you right that second? You'll be wanted for kidnapping. I take it the airboat was stolen from their docks? By sunrise, someone will be looking for you." She hoped that would take care of it.

He asked, "I'm not good enough for you, huh?"

"No, Ricky, you're not good enough for you. You really just want me to make you look good."

His mouth just hung open.

The first smear of gray dawn showed. On the eastern shore dead ahead was a gas-phone-dockage-motel sign, black on dirty-white. One little white light bulb hung over it. She would get a rental car and head back north for State Road 520 where it crosses the St. Johns and try to salvage things. She suggested he get off the river quickly, too, but head south. She didn't have to add to head for momma and daddy's. He might be running for his life.

CHAPTER SEVEN

As first light edged up in the east, the St. Johns River was still gray, dark, chilly, and misty.

You are hungry, aren't you, Clayt? I was awake, and my stomach growled. I noted on the chart I camped at a place just north of the Pine Island Resort, eastern shore of southern Lake George. I needed a nice big restaurant breakfast. I unzipped my sleeping bag, rolled it up, doused the fire, packed the tent, and shoved off.

Lights showed at the resort, so I paddled over and pulled in hoping to find a restaurant. I was starving.

I was too early. Their restaurant was empty. A young girl, likely in high school, greeted me and took my order, two over light, bacon, toast, and OJ.

"Coffee?" she asked.

I hesitated.

"Cream and sugar?"

I said, "Yeah." It sounded good for a change.

She was cute and probably headed for school by 8:30. She wore a T-shirt, FSU's colors, garnet with bright gold block letters across the chest. Those big block letters read, J-O-L-E-E-N.

"Joleen?"

She turned around to show me the back. It says, THE SOUND OF THE SOUTH! NOW AT THE LONE CABBAGE!

"The what?"

"She's terrific. The Lone Cabbage. Where she's singing. South of here. Never been there, but I love her. My older sister, she's 21, and all her friends all love Joleen. They dropped off a bunch of the Tee's, a promo, I guess, so I grabbed one."

"I'll try to stop by."

The breakfast was the right move. I was back on the water by 8:30 A.M., aiming to knock off over twenty miles.

Paddling through the headwaters of Lake George and back in the St. Johns River, I saw the river changed personality once again; it was a winding, meandering well-defined river again with tight obvious riverbanks. The plus was the channel was easy to follow; it was the whole river. The negative was, I expected more current.

By late afternoon, with Lake George behind me, I turned the corner, continuing to claw my way south, approaching the little towns of Astor on the river's western shore and Volusia east.

The birds were up, individuals and flocks everywhere. It was a good sign regarding the weather, a good forecast. A hawk, dark against the lighter sky, high, came from behind me, wings flapping hard in a hurry. Then he was gone southbound. Less than five minutes later, looked like the same bird headed back, a red- shouldered hawk, wings flapping even harder, because there was a large fish hanging out of each side of his beak. He hurried, doing his job, to feed a bunch of little gaping mouths screeching in the nest. Somehow, the sight gave me a push.

I was talking to myself again. It was hard not to, pretty much alone in that still, raw, desolate wilderness. A swamp is a swamp. Maybe talking to myself a little was to be expected.

I should think ahead to the next campsite. There was still plenty of light. Dusk fades to dark in a blink out here, and there's nothing darker than being at water level in a swamp at night.

I finally slid under the State Road 46 bridge. SR 46 is a good mileage marker; it means I was nearly as far south as Titusville. The St. Johns is up to a quarter mile wide and on a course nearly straight north and south. I had a nice stroke going, nice feathering and shoulder turns. I wasn't even tired. From the looks of things, I guessed, a campsite for this night would have to wait 'til I was well below what's ahead.

That's what concerned me, the place called Lake Puzzle.

I paddled through the lake's mouth. What was ahead as far as I could see, it is aptly named.

After paddling hard all the way from the bridge, racing the clock south, my paddle was suddenly dead in the water.

I said, " Now this is a puzzle!" The sound of my voice didn't even echo.

There was no St. Johns River; it was gone. What opened up in front of me looked like a gigantic version of a handheld fan spread open over miles. What was the river dribbled out in thousands of forks, shallow creeks, dead-ended meanders, and oxbows.

Everything for miles looked choked by long colonies of floating vegetation, hyacinths, and one near to me, the rare, flowery, spatterdock with its ivory-colored, ball-shaped blooms. Even the swamp grass was different; it was called cord grass. It was tall, looking like brooms, and clusters of bristles trying to sweep the sky, with long broom handles jammed into the muck.

The place teemed with life, insects, flies, and thousands of wading birds. Guide books showed more of them here than any place in Florida.

My view was a nearly infinite distant horizon, surrounding an equally distant, flat, still, featureless, pockmarked, shimmering hot mirror.

The Fisherman's Guide Book describes this as a primordial flood plain, meaning ancient, older than even Florida.

That part of the St. Johns is literally as old as it looks, almost unchanged since the whole peninsula rose up around it out of the sea.

The going was slow.

How did explorers here ever find the way before GPS, charts, fishing maps, and guide books? A dead-ended creek can look just like the channel should look and not expose its ruse for four or five miles; that's eight or ten miles backtracking without an inch of headway.

I watched the slight movement of the hyacinths; it's a way to tell the direction of a slow current. I put the paddle across the deck in front of me and reached down and plucked a dead leaf from a floater. Dropping it in the clear showed direction.

It inched south to north.

If I go perpendicular to the current, I should eventually find a channel.

My paddle even touched bottom several times.

Then it dawned on me. This was perfect country for that one very-popular, very-special bird, the airboat.

This was airboat country. It was shallow and grassy. The limited high ground was wet. It was surrounded by nearby populated urban hotspots, Titusville, Orlando, Cocoa, and Cape Canaveral. It was Friday afternoon. Folks were out of work, maybe even early, anxious to get out there and have some fun and enjoy nature.

I realized the flaw in my thinking. Going perpendicular could leave me broadsided.

The farther south I progressed, the more prevalent the airboats would become, not just the ones roaring out of the tall grass and across open water, but that hidden one. Each was skippered by a responsible, trained master who would constantly search forward for that little flag on a hidden pole of a low-sitting kayak, dead-quiet in the water?

I don't think so.

There was no high ground in sight. I wouldn't know where to camp out here, but I knew there had to be somewhere up ahead soon. Wildlife and wading birds were everywhere, congregating all over that bayou-like world. That meant a food supply; and that meant snails for one thing, wading birds' favorites, and generations of shells piling up, and that meant shell middens on high ground.

I thought I should congratulate myself for all that analytical thinking, but I just paddled on. I kept telling myself, *I'll get there.*

I kept thinking I heard thunderous roars in the distance, the mowing down of cord grass.

I didn't have long to wait.

What I heard was different, not the distant throbbing roar of aircraft-style propellers. Except for what I heard, it was all silent hereabouts.

I heard laughter, excited, shrieking, loud, mob laughter.

I paddled and feathered quietly around a stand of tall grass, and there it was: a huge airboat, dead in the water, heeling way over toward me with more than a dozen excited passengers. They were all jammed on the near side of the vessel, jumping up and down, laughing, yelling, screaming, and pointing at the water.

I counted the airboat's seats. Four rows rose fore to aft like bleachers at a football game. Four padded seats per row. At the top were three more passengers plus the pilot. That was sixteen in all aboard a 25-foot flat-bottomed scow.

In the water, laid out in front of them, thrashing, mouth wide open and mad as hell was a big gray 'gator, ten feet long, four hundred pounds of pure predator.

They never even noticed me slipping past. I paddled silently, feathering the blades without making a ripple as fast as I could go. I couldn't imagine that thing, an airboat like a bus, roaring at me out of the dead of night. I've read that night is air boater's favorite time, the thrill of thrills.

Come the weekend on the St. Johns, I would face a whole different real Florida.

I paddled through the darkness, head lamp on, poking through the night mist, bright-green chem sticks lashed fore and one aft atop my flag pole. It was getting late, past midnight. I passed the Lone Cabbage Restaurant and Fish Camp, and it was dark. Just past was Mulberry Mound, not a managed campsite, but it got the nod in the guide book. It's high and dry.

I was still eighty plus miles north of the St. John's headwaters, Blue Cypress Lake in Indian River County, the end of the beginning, I guessed one could call it. I wondered what this whole journey would mean when it was all behind me. I was even beginning to ask questions like, "Why am I, or any of us, here at all?"

It was like the Living Florida is saying, "Cut down all our trees to make your lumber, pave over the greenery, litter with your plastic and garbage, and Florida will take away your fresh water and parch your throats."

At best, so far, it seemed my eyes were opening wider and wider. This Florida was real, a delicate balance, interdependent, each facet knitted to the next, a dropped stitch here and there, it all unravels.

As I lay in my tent, listening to the sounds of the St. Johns River at night, eons of shells, generation after generation, form the ground under me. I closed my eyes.

CHAPTER EIGHT

A taxi from Cocoa pulled off what the driver called Kingston Road, SR 520, just east of the bridge over the St. Johns River, made a half U-turn on the edge of the parking lot, and stopped as close to the front door as one could get. He was pretty sure the young lady gave him a wrong address, the Lone Cabbage Restaurant & Fish Camp. He turned to the back seat with a questioning look on his face.

Then, he realized. Open-mouthed, he broke into a broad smile and said, "I'm glad you're alright, Miss Jackson."

Joleen rolled her eyes. "Guess everybody knows, huh?"

"Well, from Seminole to Orange to here in Brevard County, yeah, we all heard about your kidnapping. Everybody's been worried for you."

"It was all really nothing, just a big stupid nothing, really. He was just misconstruing a lot of things, just upset." She fumbled with both her words and her hands in her jean's pockets fishing for crumpled dollar bills, loose change, anything. She didn't have a dime. "Oh my, um, oh dear. I'm so sorry for causing all this, and thank you all so much. What do I owe you?"

The driver reached over and slapped the meter lever to "off ." "Not this time, Missy." He was out of the driver's door and opening her door before she could argue.

"You don't have to do that, please."

"The day you opened here, Miss Jackson, do you have any idea how many fares I had that day, Orlando to here, Cocoa Beach to here, Rockledge, Merritt Island, Canaveral, and then back again? I even took the foursome home whose airboat got swiped."

Joleen just stood there in her same wrinkled jeans and sequined black T-shirt she wore when kidnapped, biting her lip, fighting back tears.

He returned to his cab door, yanked it open, turned, and slipped behind the wheel. He rolled down the window. "I wish you all the luck in the world." After maneuvering the second half of that U-turn, he was gone.

Joleen watched the cab climb back on SR 520 and keep rolling back east toward Cocoa Beach.

At least her car was still there, parked down by the rear kitchen entrance, right in front of the trash bins. It wasn't up on blocks, as she'd envisioned, and the tires were still on all four wheels. Her luggage, from the first day she'd arrived here, clean clothes, cosmetics, money, and credit cards were, she hoped, still in the trunk.

She pulled open the restaurant's heavy front door and stepped inside. Standing right there, blocking the entrance, was the manager, hands on hips and with closed fists.

Instantly his face broke open in a huge grin. He said, "Welcome home, Joleen. Welcome home, Sweetheart."

Overwhelmed, Joleen fell into his open arms, sobbing. She shuddered and trembled. "Oh, Harvey," she managed between sobs.

"We were so damned worried that we'd find your body face-down in the St. Johns River. The bosses will be mad as hornets about your "friend" running off with you, terrorizing the place, and scaring everybody. They had to eat all those dinner and drink checks, thousands of dollars. They couldn't charge the customers after all of that when you just walked out.

"A ten-thousand-dollar airboat was stolen right under our noses from our own docks. All the promo money to introduce you gone, wasted. We're looking bad, real bad, is how the bosses see it. There'll be questions. I'm sure everything will work out, but you're going to have to have some answers, real ones, honest ones. We'll have to have a little talk. The sheriff is going to want to talk to you. I'll have to let them know you're here. There are "John Doe" charges out there for who did it and why. Joleen, who was it?"

Joleen caught her breath, stopped sniffling, settled down and listened. Harvey was dead serious. She wouldn't and couldn't answer. Maybe when she got some rest. She'd think about the charges and maybe even dropping them. If dropping charges made it all look like nothing but "love," so be it, but it was nothing like love. The truth was already haunting her. She'd just have to think it through. One question prevailed. How could she hide, when she sang in public places for a living, from someone determined to either have her or kill her?

Harvey concluded. "We'll want you to stay with us temporarily. We'll be adding security and new rules about coming and going, but you'll be safe."

She was shown what had at one time been the old boss' bedroom, with its lockable door separating it from the adjacent private office. She could stay there as long as she needed.

Joleen took the keys he held out. The room had an outer door to the parking lot and a main door that opened up on the great dining hall with its small, circular bandstand up against the huge sliding glass walls overlooking the patio. On the other side of the dining room was the front bar.

Her room came with a walk-in closet for performers' costumes, hanging outfits, storage for instrument cases, luggage, plus a genuine-looking theatrical vanity complete with wrap- around bright light bulbs. Joleen thought the vanity was perfect. Completing the accommodations was a very comfortable-looking queen adjustable bed, dresser, big TV and two comfy-looking lounge chairs.

She hauled in her luggage from the parking lot, put things away, hung up her outfits, and showered. Toweling off, she felt weak, as fatigue caught up with her.

She thought she'd nap for just an hour, but the time whizzed by. All she did was think.

What if I file for dismissal of the charges? Will he leave me alone? What if, when I'm interviewed, I give the cops his name? The parents will call out the heavy power, the biggest, high-dollar attorneys in the country. They could flat out offer double or triple the value of that airboat. Bribes? They could promise huge money to squelch it all. Even with a conviction, they could pressure for minimal, or even no, zero jail. There'd be the promise to return the stolen airboat or replace it. Probation only? Probation and a fine? Any slap on the wrist could anger him and deeply embarrass and humiliate his parents. A Wentworth with a record? They could come after me. He could. He could snap, "She's mine or no one's." Stuff like that happens all the time.

She dozed off for an hour and rose up groggy, finally moved to the vanity, and stared at the mirror. She finished doing her eyes and put on lip gloss. Prepping for her rehearsal, she slipped on a fitted radiant shade of navy turtleneck with long sleeves, white Levis, and blue Topsider sandals.

She called the trio in Orlando. They leapt for joy and said they'd be there by five or six-ish.

She thought, *Well, you're back singin' on the river!*

She could handle this. It was nothing. *Just like I told the taxi driver.*

She stepped out the front door to check with Harvey that the bandstand had a hot mic and a CD player ready to play her music-only discs. She made sure the speakers were up and her single, ceiling-mounted, pin key light was working.

He stood near the end of the bar, his customary rehearsal post. The electrical panel was right around the corner, with the panel doors open. The room would usually be empty until staff set-up for dinner. She definitely preferred it that way, empty, except for the audience of one, Harvey. She rehearsed better when the room was dark and silent, and she was alone.

She asked, "You have someone in the house over there I don't know? Thought this room was closed, 2 to 5."

The young man came up from the docks, across the patio, and in through a glass door cut in the whole wall of glass. He was immediately met by Harvey. Harvey questioned him, mostly to make sure he wasn't the kidnapper back again. He had no idea what the kidnapper looked like. The young man said he'd come a long way, heard good things, even saw her name featured on a T-shirt, and wondered if and when she'd be singing.

Harvey smiled.

Clayt extended his right hand and said, "I'm Clayt McIver from Welaka."

The manager eyed him, studying Clayt's face. "McIver? Larry McIver's son?"

"Yes, Sir. Lawrence McIver is my father."

"Sure enough. Long-time citrus guy up there, right?"

Clayt nodded.

Harvey went on, "I'm from Ocala. Got a cousin in Palatka, close friend of Larry's. I've met your father. Fine man. Tell him Harvey Streetman said hello."

Clayt said, "Well, citrus is down, what with the Greening disease. My dad suggested I get in the kayak and head south, hopefully find a job, go all the way to Blue Cypress Lake if I need to, so that's what I'm doing."

"Well, no son of Lawrence McIver is gonna get stuck in the mud, that's for sure." Satisfied, he sat Clayt at a table for two right next to the bandstand. He told Clayt about Joleen's frightening story, at least, as he knew it. She was kidnapped right off the bandstand and dragged out onto the river in the dark of night in a stolen airboat.

Harvey noted Joleen was piqued at the interruption. "He came to hear you sing, Joleen!"

She noted the visitor was disheveled. Though nice enough looking, he needed a haircut. Sun-bleached blond, he was freshly clean shaven with a tanned face and arms.

His tan shirt and tan shorts gave him an outdoorsman's look.

Harvey's eyes followed hers across the room. "This young fellow just paddled by kayak most of the entire St. Johns River, single-handedly, some 250 miles. Paddling! Himself! Alone! For days! All the way from up near Jacksonville here and, from here, he's heading all the way south to the actual headwaters, all the way down into Indian River County! His name is, Clayton McIver from Welaka."

She slowly nodded. *That boy's gotta be some athlete*, she thought. She liked people who challenged themselves, like she did. It took courage to do what he was doing, same way it took courage for her to get on stage every time she did it.

The manager added, "He said he won't make a sound. We won't even know he's here, and you know what? He asked if we had Stella Artois on tap. I ordered him one, and he's been just enjoying—a cold one is probably a rarity for him—and relaxing, just calmly waiting ever since."

"Oh. Well, now." She approved that the Lone Cabbage was carrying Stella, the fine Belgian Lager, and the young man who ordered it. She headed for the bandstand by way of his table.

Right next to it, she stumbled, turned her ankle, and cried out, "Ouch."

Clayt stood. "Whoa! Did you hurt yourself? Here. Sit down for a minute. Is it swelling? Can I get you some ice, Miss Jackson?"

"Thanks. No swelling that I can see, but I won't be surprised if it swells up later."

"Oh, poor thing. I know that hurts worse than anything."

Joleen limped over to the chair he moved out from the table. "Hi, I'm Joleen."

"Clayt."

The waiter came to the table. "Anything I can get you?" he asked.

"I'll have another Stella and...." Clayt gestured to Joleen who was examining her ankle.

As the waiter turned to her, she looked up. "I'll have one of those," she said, nodding at the Stella glass Clayt held.

He looked at her and smiled

She looked back at him and couldn't help but notice his eyes were blue as a Florida sky. She laughed sheepishly. "Some spectacle I'm making of myself."

He smiled more broadly at her.

Clayt, observing her, noted she didn't appear to be shaken up in the least. On the contrary, she was as elegant as a lady turning her ankle could be.

"Well, I was about to start rehearsing. Stay if you'd like. I don't mind."

"I'd like that," he said, looking at her.

Joleen's head picked up slightly as she glanced at this stranger. He had a nice, calm way about him. He seemed real. She smiled at him even before she knew she would.

The waiter returned and placed a sparkling glass of Stella before her.

Joleen slid the disc into the CD player. The mic came up, and her long black eyelashes closed. Joleen's voice floated across the room and out onto the patio, the large, outdoor speakers spreading it once again across the sun-streaked St. Johns.

She sang song after song. The last one was an Eric Clapton classic, *Nobody Loves You When You're Down And Out*. Clayt knew of it. It was that last verse that would last and last.

Listening for more than an hour, he felt he never heard anything like it.

Her voice was clear and throaty. When she turned away holding the mic, her sound drifted into the distance. Those notes seemed magical. Mesmerized by her voice, he thought she was beautiful.

CHAPTER NINE

I chose what I thought was a perfect moment.

She delivered out across the room, in one last silken whisper, the last word of the last lyric of the last song.

It had to be around 10 O'clock.

At the bar, every head, those on every stool and every one standing three deep, turned as if commanded and faced the bandstand. Shouts, whistles, and applause rang out. The room was at full capacity. The diners rose, one after another, applauding in a standing ovation and begging for an encore.

She raised her head in appreciation. She was truly striking in a delicate lace white tunic, white satin wide-leg pants and sleek, sky-blue leather heels with sparkling ankle straps, sore ankle be damned.

The overhead key light made her teary eyes sparkle. Her lips closed, and, with the mic held in her fingers, she let her arm drop to her side. She smiled and turned to the audience, first on her right, my side, nodding thanks, and then, to her left, the same gesture plus a thrown kiss with her back to me.

I quietly clicked open the glass door and clicked it closed behind me. She never heard or saw me leave. There was nothing I could say that she had not heard a thousand times. I hoped not leaving a note with some stupid come-on or a business card requesting an exchange of phone numbers, might make her realize I'm real. I would actually try to catch up to her somehow, once again, soon.

I crossed the patio, dropped down onto the docks extending out into the St. Johns, and dropped into the kayak's cockpit.

I went to uncleat my mooring line with just one hand, extending my arm, attempting to unwrap the little figure eights from around the dock cleat, but I couldn't quite bring myself to do it; my hand slowly sank into the river water up to my forearm.

That mooring line was the only real connection left. I wondered if I would ever see her again.

I felt suddenly very alone.

I uncleated the mooring line, pulled it in, coiled it, and stowed it. I was drifting north in the dark on the slow, but relentless, St. Johns current, the paddle crosswise on the deck in front of me. There wasn't a sound, not a single living thing moving, just the current. Drifting simply didn't seem to matter, even though I was losing ground that was so hard won. Losing was just another form of being lost, and I was lost. I had to snap out of it.

Under only the moon, I put one blade in, stroked it, feathered it, then the other, sought the shallows on the western side of the river, and headed south toward nearby Mulberry Mound, my campsite of yesterday. I tucked myself into the north point of Mulberry, the opposite end from where I camped, putting myself in the lee of the river current. I sat there, curled up in my cocoon until dawn.

I could have sullenly gone back to the Lone Cabbage for lunch at breakfast time, since they don't open for breakfast, but I was afraid my delicious memories would seem too real.

I moved to the Mulberry Mound's south shore. I set up the same camp, built the same fire, and cooked breakfast, the last of eggs, bacon, buttered toast, and coffee, and built up resolve. Next would come the last leg. I prayed it would be an end of a beginning.

I would call home next chance.

Why don't you just call right now? Or as soon as you can find cell service?

No, because then it would no longer be a secret that there's a hole in my life. One childish high-school female friend and even college girlfriends were only the dalliances of pretending kids. There would be no hiding that I am, for sure, all shook up. This hour, this minute of this day, the one job I have is to launch this kayak southbound and place one blade after another in this St. Johns River... and paddle... paddle... paddle.

CHAPTER TEN

"Morning Sweetheart!" Manager Harvey rapped on Joleen's door at nine o'clock in the morning. "You want the good news first or the bad?"

"Go away," she answered through the door.

"Come on, Joleen, which will it be?"

"The good."

"OK then. Last night's gross take was an all-time high record for the Lone Cabbage. And that ain't draft beer! Management is delirious. You did it, Sweetheart."

She yanked open her door, wearing beige pants and matching light sweater. "What's the bad?"

He bit his lower lip, then said, "The sheriff's here."

"Shit."

"He's waiting for you next door in the office. Seems very nice...."

Joleen groaned, "Uh-huh. I'll be right there."

She clicked the door shut and stood there staring back at it, then crossed to the vanity and plunked down on the stool in front of the mirror. She knew what the obvious questions would be, but she had no clue as to the right answers. *Maybe he'll be helpful. Probably not.* She grabbed her lip gloss, willed her hand to stop trembling, applied the nude-pink color, blotted, and gave the mirror a nod. She stood, inhaled deeply, and walked out the door into the office next door.

"Ah, Miss Jackson, a pleasure to meet you,"

He wasn't at all what she expected. He wasn't bald with a paunch or coasting near retirement. There was no baggy suit with shiny backside from years of sliding across squad-room chairs and patrol car seats.

"Thanks," was the best she could muster.

He was 6'4, and had jet-black hair, big, black eyebrows, and, though freshly clean shaven, sported a bluish shadow over a pleasant white face.

"If you have a minute, Miss Jackson? We need to talk."

She took instant inventory, jacket, badge, boots. He wore a black leather jacket with a big silver star over his heart, gray chinos, and shiny black motorcycle boots.

"Please, sit down. Relax." Standing between the two captain's chairs on each side out front of the big executive desk, he gestured to one. "I'm Tom Mackey, Deputy Detective, Brevard County Sheriff's Office."

Joleen sat on the front edge of the chair on his right and said, "Yes, Sir. Thank you.... I'm Joleen."

He remained standing. "You have a tough decision to make, Joleen. May I call you Joleen?"

"Yes, please, sir, Joleen, Detective Mackey."

"How about you call me Tom, OK? Now, there are charges pending in this case to which you have direct involvement, kidnapping, theft of more than twelve thousand dollars in property, the airboat. We need an alleged perpetrator name and location, if possible."

She was unable to say anything. Her eyes moved up from his chest to his face.

"Joleen, let me explain. If this alleged kidnapping is, in actuality, a lover's quarrel, it would be understandable that you might want to protect his name, perhaps even wish to see kidnapping charges dropped.

"The theft remains, and you find yourself left in one of two uncomfortable positions, accomplice or co-conspirator."

"It was no lover's quarrel," she whispered.

"Should you state you <u>don't</u> know him but actually <u>do</u> know him, you're back in one of those two uncomfortable positions. The truth will out, as he is interrogated, and you will have possibly perjured yourself."

"Oh, I know him. He desperately wants to be in love, have an exclusive girlfriend, and make future plans, but it just wasn't true. He didn't love me, and I sure didn't love him; he just loved the texting, the calling. Disturbing. He wanted to own me. It was scary."

"I can certainly understand if you know the individual, and are afraid he might want revenge, that you might be frightened. Your fears are justifiable. It happens. Example: He's in love, but you're not. He goes over the edge."

"He just thought he was."

"And you reasoned with him while he raced through the night on the St. Johns in a stolen airboat."

"I guess you could say that."

"A court order could be issued at any time, Joleen, wherein an individual is prohibited by law from contacting you in any form. Penalties for violation are harsh. You know that?"

"I know, Sir, but they aren't perfect."

"You tell me if I'm right: you think if you withhold his name and insist on dropping the kidnap charge that he might just let you alone? Fact is, should you reveal his name, you can drop any charges pending as to your kidnapping. When we pick him up, the loss victims and your contract employers here at the Lone Cabbage will file the theft complaint against him. He'll be arrested under Florida Law, jailed pending bail, indicted, and eventually have his day in court."

"I understand."

"He has a name, Joleen... and address, location."

"He chained me to the seat in that airboat."

"I'm not surprised, Joleen."

"I'm afraid of him and his parents. They're prominent, and he'll have embarrassed them. They'll bring on the big-money power attorneys, try for probation, a fine; they could blame me and come after me."

"The Lone Cabbage owners will provide you with 'round- the- clock protection, monitor all comings and goings; I believe they already told you they put on extra security. They've already contacted their longtime attorneys, who have represented them for years, to represent them in the theft matter. That airboat was docked here at the Lone Cabbage private docks by Lone Cabbage customers."

He paused. "They love success. They love you, Joleen."

He looked at his watch but didn't seem in a rush to get the name immediately. He was willing to wait. He held out his calling card to her. "Don't hesitate to call."

"Richard Randolph Wentworth III, nickname Ricky."

"Best idea of location?"

"The parents."

Detective Mackey nodded, turned toward the door, and said, "Thank you, Joleen." He hesitated, then said, "Oh! I'm told you knock that Jake Owen song right out of the ballpark!" He smiled ear-to-ear at her. The office door closed, and he was gone.

She heard him open the front door, heard him close it quietly, with care, then the roar of a Harley, throwing gravel, as he blew out of the Lone Cabbage parking lot and hit SR 520 burning rubber.

When she stood to leave, her bruised ankle gave her a little twinge, oddly a reminder. She thought of the sun-drenched stranger who had kayaked all those miles down the St. Johns.

CHAPTER ELEVEN

Despite my determination last night to put paddle to water by dawn, my getaway to the next destination, Camp Holly, was sluggish. I was sluggish, even dragging. I knew nothing of Camp Holly except that the guidebook shows "Restaurant." and anything will beat what I have left aboard. I might call home when I get there. It might cheer me up. My I-phone was on my portable charger just in case, good for 80 hours, so they say, and that was the first plug-in. It should be fine.

My paddles hit water at 10:00 A.M.

I figured six hours at my usual speed, about four pm. My first stroke swept the St. Johns north. The late May sun already made the channel surface shine. Endless-looking stretches of tall grass on all sides were glazed over by heat waves horizon to horizon. It was amazing how vast Florida's swamplands are and how they can look like bronzed rolling oceans.

Stopping to rest would only make time and distance back up. My mind kept backing up to last night. I could hear that last song as if from a speaker in my ear. Sometimes I almost saw Joleen's face reflected in the waters, as I tried to put both the image and the water behind me. I knew there were miles and miles before me.

I bore down, paddle to water for six hours, for fourteen miles, and I was where I wanted to be. The St. Johns takes a slight bend here, west just north of the SR 192 bridge, west of West Melbourne. Over on the east shore, where the inside bend is all tall grass, palm, scrub growth, and floating vegetation, I saw the upper half of the wooden viewing tower and the thatched roof of the tiki bar at Camp Holly.

I followed the bend of the channel, and Camp Holly came into full view. It sits almost at sea level at the bottom of a hill that forms the bridge rise. Over the bridge, SR 192 crosses the St. Johns.

Apparently, Camp Holly once offered rental cabins for campers. Some cabins remained. It looked like they were used for airboat maintenance, repairs, and parts. Other newer-looking buildings were scattered about to create a tiny community. There was a restaurant, ticket office, souvenir shop, and restrooms. The tiki bar in the center of its own pavilion with wood rail overlooked the airboats comings and goings and dockage activity.

Up on the rise of SR 192, a large sign on a tall pole read "Camp Holly-Airboat Rides." Their entrance road off the highway sloped steeply down to a bleached-white gravel parking lot. Its west end slanted down and dipped into the river via a very wide, wet-gray, concrete airboat ramp. The ramp was at least 75 feet wide, wide enough that two airboat-sized crafts could be launched from trailers and hauled out at the same time.

I figured to beach my kayak more or less center on the ramp and drag it to the side out of the way. They would be closing soon, and I'd only be there, probably, less than an hour.

I turned my bow to approach the ramp. Off to my left, close to the main building, isolated from the public by a ten-foot-tall chain-link fence with gates to each of four airboat docks, an airboat captain hunched over his aircraft-style engine, preparing for his next excursion into the St. Johns' swamplands.

There was some current, but I was right on course to beach softly.

Suddenly, looking up, I blinked. I thought my eyes were betraying me.

Sixty-odd feet or so in front of me, standing shin-deep on the ramp, was a small child. Her wild mop of hair, like a past-bloom dandelion, was shaggy and filthy-looking. A nightshirt-type garment, probably once white, hung from little shoulders to little knees.

I was closer. She was seven or eight, dirty but cute little face and dark eyes. She waved at me—no, waved to me—asking me to come to her. I heard her call out, *"Puedo ir contigo?"*

The airboat captain, hearing her, looked up from his airboat beyond the fence, and saw the little girl on the ramp. He turned in my direction and shouted across the way, "Hey, she's talking Spanish. She wants to come with you!"

Hearing his remark, I blinked again, trying to see what was in front of me more clearly. I wondered out loud, "Where are the parents? Where's her mother?" I called out to the airboat captain, "Have you seen any parents?"

The captain shrugged. "Haven't noticed. Busy. See the signs?" He pointed at the big red signs on the fence every ten feet, CHILDREN UNDER 18 MUST BE ACCOMPANIED BY ADULTS.

My bow touched bottom on the ramp next to the little girl. Her cheeks were glossy from tears. I stepped out of the kayak, and she lunged at me and wrapped her arms around my one leg and hugged me with all her might.

My mouth hung open. She clung to me. I shout at the airboat captain, "Think in the Restaurant?"

The airboat captain stopped what he was doing, turned around, still holding a wrench, and stepped onto the little boarding dock next to his airboat. "Ya know," he cleared his throat and spoke up loudly, "was a big old Greyhound-type bus up on 192 from the east. Old, white-washed-looking paint job, even the windows, black letters on the side, said, 'Southern Academy,' coulda been a buncha druggies ya ask me."

I looked from him to her.

"I heard the air brakes squeal and hiss. It stopped next to our sign and did a huge U-turn, took several efforts, and headed off back where it came from."

I read drug traffickers and the like on I-95 check to see if they're being followed, pull off, like on a SR192, and cruise awhile, then, all clear, get back up on I-95 and keep trucking north. Human trafficking's a major problem.

"I didn't put the two things together at the time. Next thing I notice, that little tyke comes from behind the highway guardrails. She could have been hiding now that I think about it, and sort of skipped down our driveway and across the parking lot, barefoot!"

My stomach churned. "What's your name, Sweetheart? Where's your mommy?"

She said nothing but let go of my leg.

She shook her shaggy head. "*Mi nombre es Maya Muñoz .*"

I managed to translate. Her name was Maya something. "What are you doing out here all alone, Maya?" I hoped maybe her parents were at the restaurant. "Let's go inside, Maya. I'd like an ice cream cone. Would you?"

I took her hand, and we walked to the front door. She never took her eyes off me.

The waitress, keys in hand, met us, her hand on the door knob. "Sorry, we're closing up now."

"Miss, there's no one inside? Are you sure?"

She seemed to see I had a problem. "Yes, Sir. What's the problem?"

"She doesn't seem to have any parents. Wandered down off 192. Doesn't seem to even be from around here. Name is Maya."

The little voice is almost a whisper. "*Baje del bus para el bano. El bus se fue sin mi. El bus olia muy mal. Yo queria huir.*"

The waitress said, "Oh my, she says she got off the bus to go to the bathroom. The bus went away, and the bus smelled extremely bad. That she wanted to run away."

I was relieved the waitress knew Spanish. "I'm Clayt McIver. She was standing on the ramp."

"I'm Diana."

"Could we sit down a minute? I think we have to call someone and get some help."

"Of course, please come in. Sit down."

"Maya and I thought we'd have an ice cream cone, didn't we?"

Diana said, "I bet you like chocolate, Maya. Will you help me?" Taking Maya's hand, she moved over to the counter. "I'd call 911," she said over her shoulder.

I pulled my cell phone out of my pocket, scrolled my list, and started punching in numbers. "I'm sure there's a deputy somewhere around I-95 and SR 192. I'm calling the sheriff."

I listened to the dispatcher answer and said, "I'm Clayt McIver. I'm kayaking on the St. Johns and stopped here at Camp Holly. I think I've discovered a child who may have escaped from human trafficking. I think she slipped away from a bus when she had the chance. Speaks only Spanish. Little girl. We're here at Camp Holly, SR 192 just north of the bridge over the St. Johns River."

"Address?"

"Ah yes, just a …. "

"That's OK. Got it. A patrol deputy is in the sector. Be on scene ten to fifteen minutes. Recommend stay sheltered, out of sight. Over."

"Thanks. We'll wait in the front building, the restaurant."

"Very good. Deputy Lieutenant Ross Partee will be contacting you at this number. No further, out."

I punched disconnect but held the phone.

Diana handed Maya and me each a chocolate cone. She added, "Good call."

Ten minutes went by, as we sat and waited. My heart was colder than the ice cream, as I imagine what Maya might have been through.

The deputy called to affirm our location.

Diana wiped Maya's face with a wet warm cloth while she quizzed her, the name of her town, family, brothers, and sisters.

Then we heard a distant siren. We yanked open the front door, keys still in the lock jangling, and stood in the doorway.

The deputy stepped quickly toward us, lights flashing.

"I'm Lieutenant Ross Partee, Deputy Detective in charge, Child Crime. What's going on?"

I introduced us. "I'm Clayt McIver. This is Diana, Camp Holly staff, and this is little Maya Muñoz.

Diana said, "I asked her, she said, *'Mi pueblo es Cartagena,' a coastal town, and 'Yo soy de Colombia.' Colombia, S.A., South America.*"

The Lieutenant nodded.

I asked, "What's the procedure, Lieutenant?"

"I'll transport her to our complex. En route, I'll contact FDC, Florida Department Child and Families section covering the tri-county area. They'll take charge of the child. They'll contact the reciprocal Colombian agency, who will attempt to contact any parents or relatives. Hopefully, with success, a representative of the United States will escort little Maya home."

"What will you need from me?"

"Your contact, Mister McIver, spelling of your name, address, phone. You'll likely be called to document how you discovered the alleged. It's pretty obvious, I'm sorry to say. If Maya can go home, great. She might well have been just playing in front of her house in Cartagena, Colombia, when abducted. Traffickers love coastal towns. There are countless little children, once trafficked, never heard from again."

"Thank you, Lieutenant." I couldn't help but give Maya a little hug.

"We thank <u>you</u> for being alert to what might be happening, recognizing it, and taking action. Thank <u>you</u>, Mister McIver."

The deputy led little Maya to the squad car. She would ride in front with him. At the car door, she stopped, turned back, her soft little face looking at me, at us.

Diana said, "She's smiling at you, Mister McIver."

CHAPTER TWELVE

Sometimes she felt she was a prisoner. The virtual lockdown and twenty-four-hour surveillance, security always in the shadows, finally got to her.

She started running in the early morning, pioneered a trail along the outer perimeters of the Lone Cabbage property. She started in the NW corner at the fish camp, tucked under and beyond the SR 520 bridge, jogged past the floating docks of fishing boats, the full bearded, shiny-red fishermen-faces and their smiling eyes, as they cheered. Filleting knives paused in mid slice, and her white running shoes, short shorts, and T-shirt were a blur.

She swung south down to the fuel docks and snack shed. The boating customers stared while trying to pay for their fuel, and while they ogled, change for dollar bills slipped through their fingers into the shallow St. Johns waters. The glimpse of her, once again, was all but gone. Jogging on, she whipped past the screened back door of the kitchen, where the potato peelers and broccoli washers gathered outside to escape the interior heat. They stood up off their stools, raised fists, and chanted praises.

Finally, she huffed and puffed her way up the bridge rise to parallel SR 520. She laughed out loud, as the passing morning truckers blew their air horns in salute, "GO-JO- YAH! GO-JO-AH-YAH!" as they roared by, hurling back clouds of shell-mound dust.

First days it was not over 5 to 6 laps, maybe a mile, but then she worked up to 18 to 20 laps, a good five miles. She wasn't out of breath. She was calm, felt *bring it on*, ready, ready for anything, well, almost anything, except... she just wasn't ready for the phone call.

"We found it!" It was the voice of Sheriff's Deputy Detective Tom Mackey. "Thought you should know."

She had just gotten out of a long hot shower, cooled and toweled, in red-rose tailored Bermuda shorts and light, crisp linen open-collared shirt. She slipped on sandals. "The airboat?"

"Yup."

"Where?"

"Not two miles north of where you jumped ship. He apparently stepped onto a dock, gave it a shove, set it adrift in the St. Johns current, and never looked back."

Instantly she wondered, *Will they drop the theft charges*? "Is it back with the owners?"

"Impounded, pending."

"Pending what?"

"Evidence gathering, prints, search for firearms, drugs, disposition of the charges, could be as much as grand theft, first degree due enhancements, the kidnapping."

"Meaning?"

"Subject to adjudication, grand theft third-degree would be just for value like the airboat up to twenty grand, enhanced due to use in a kidnapping. The theft could mean five years plus fines, up to thirty years imprisonment plus fines. Involving adult kidnapping, could go to first degree felony, can mean life imprisonment, thousands in fines. Whatever way it goes, he's through."

"You're saying you got him?"

The pause was indicative. "Well, he's still at large, but...."

"As I've said before, and I'll say it one more time, Detective Mackey. He's spoiled. He gets his way. He wanted a hot car, daddy got him one. He wanted an airboat, he just took it. You don't know him. He's out there. If he knows the charges, he'll be mad, resentful. He won't stop. He'll find me."

The side of her throat started throbbing. "The point is, you haven't got him." Her fingertips pushed on the throb. "What about the parents?"

"They claim they're shocked. Can't be. Refuse to believe it."

She sensed doubt in his voice.

"They insist they have no idea of his whereabouts. They claim, in fact, to be concerned that he's been missing and not showing up, as he periodically would, for Sunday dinners on the lanai. He does so loves them.'"

"Did you look under their guest room bed?"

"It's only a matter of time, Joleen. Just relax. You're in good hands. He'll show, Joleen. You've got to be patient."

"I'm going to seek counsel to ask if I can drop the kidnap charge."

"All I can say is, they're not your charges, Joleen. They are the state's, filed to protect the public."

"My gig here is just about up. The Joleen R. Jackson, Lone Cabbage management-entertainer contract ends in not much more than a week!"

"We're on it. There's a BOLO out everywhere on him, description, photos. Just be aware of your surroundings. Practice looking around if you go out. Watch yourself, whatever you do. Stay home."

"OK, Tom. Fine, Tom. Thanks, Tom. Bye-bye, Tom."

I have to get up on that bandstand tonight and sing? She looked out her room's window at her car parked in the Lone Cabbage parking lot. *There might as well be bars on the windows.* She once again was her own prisoner, but this prison had no barred windows, no locks, no thick walls. *I'm simply bait.*

CHAPTER THIRTEEN

Dinner was the memory of a chocolate ice-cream cone yesterday afternoon. In the dark, I set up my popup tent down in the east corner, opposite the airboat ramp where, at one time, the campers could set up. For being so helpful, Diana cleared permission from the owner.

I was dog tired. Everything was just a jumble. I just lay there in my tent on top of my sleeping bag and stared up at nothing. Thoughts leapfrogged across my brain. Little Maya Muñoz was such a beautiful little girl. She was extremely smart and perceptive. Maya had such understanding, compassion, and a capacity for love from such a lost child. I would never be able to shake that picture of her looking back before she climbed into the patrol car. What about the last leg of this trip?

I was finally going to call home. My phone was ready to go, on charge since yesterday, and I would call them when I finished. I would say, "I made it." They'll be thrilled, but I'd keep some of the details to myself for the time being.

I flopped around all night, first on one side, then the other, then back on my back where I began. Finally, the light inside the tent changed to where I could see around me. Dawn was breaking. I wanted to be gone from Camp Holly before they opened. I gathered up my towel and shaving kit and tried the door of a former cabin-type building with a sign over it that read, "Bathrooms."

It opened, and I spotted the shower. That was a delight. I brushed my teeth and put on my last clean shorts and shirt. I downed an MRE, Meals Ready To Eat. That was another delight. It almost tasted like food for humans. I packed up, set the kayak in the water at the ramp, and shoved off.

The kayak was lighter. There was nothing in the dry ice cooler or the fresh food bin except a couple of MRE's. Going was easy. The headwaters of the St. Johns at Blue Cypress Lake are only sixteen or so miles. *I got this. It'll be a big finish.*

Two miles south of Camp Holly, the St. Johns once again turns into a beaten-down lake, this small natural one, Sawgrass Lake. I could barely spot water much less channels. It was wall-to-wall floating and submerged vegetation, not water hyacinths, rather a nonnative invasive species called hydrilla, used in hobby-type home aquariums. Apparently, some hobbyists grow tired of caring–or the goldfish die–and the whole thing, including a sprit or two of decorative hydrilla, ends up in the St. Johns. Hydrilla grows an inch per day when out in nature.

I originally thought the last leg of the voyage would end sort of triumphantly, with a grandé finalé, a crescendo, but it looked like I was going to be wrong.

The channels through Sawgrass Lake were not much wider than my kayak, so paddling was done with care, and feathering was difficult-to-impossible. The hydrilla constantly tried to catch onto the paddle blades. On the plus side, the existing channels sparkled under another beautiful blue-skied Florida day. I worked my way through the green blanket until the lake finally gave way back to its meandering river and defined banks, though narrowing, and the St. Johns continued dwindling toward the headwaters. Two kayaks moving in opposite directions would have trouble passing each other in those narrows, but I felt relentless with my goal in hand.

In just two miles was a still smaller lake with the crazy name, "Hell 'n Blazes." People exclaim, "What the hell and blazes is this?" when they try to navigate the endless floating islands of vegetation.

This whole area was the ancient sea bottom from before Florida rose up. Officially the St. Johns Flood Plain is low and flat. The drop in elevation all the way to Jacksonville is less than a yard, so the current is slow. It averages one mile an hour. The chart showed up ahead, starting a hundred years ago, dozens of canals dug supposedly to drain the swamplands and make them suitable for farming and, of course, as real estate for selling to farmers from the north interested in year-round crops. As a result, nowadays, Lake Hell 'n Blazes, is only one to two feet deep and is slowly draining away.

The so-called hydrology engineers of the 1900s seemed to forget the Florida rainy season. After they dug the canals, they levied the banks to keep the land dry. The Florida rains came right on time and re-flooded the lands up and over the banks. Boom followed by bust again.

Leaving Hell 'n Blazes in the early afternoon, I was finally back on a meandering and real-looking river, but only for two miles.

An hour past. I looked through my binoculars exactly straight true south on a manmade canal, and I couldn't see the distant far end to it. The chart showed it was six miles long and ended at the headwaters, Blue Cypress Lake. I was in Indian River County, paralleling the west border of their huge re-flooded, manmade Stick Marsh. I hunched my shoulders and pushed on, although bored with nothing to look at except the long straight canal. After paddling straight south for over hours, I finally saw the canal banks fall away.

I paddled onto the bluest, clearest, shiniest sheet of liquid glass any man could ever visit. Magnificent cypress trees line the banks and dot the lake of Blue Cypress Lake to form canopies, draping the lake's surface in sapphire-blue shadows. They stand majestically along the shorelines as well as in individual stout islands out in the lake, anchored solidly on their multiple legs with their knobby knees. They are like great, protective, androgynous warriors, at the same time, profoundly nurturing and maternal, providing the nesting homes high in their canopies to the largest concentration of osprey in the world.

This first view, as I crossed into the lake, would take anyone's breath away. It was like entering a great prehistoric wilderness, as if before Man. I was in awe of the splendor. That place made my venture not only a grand success, a singular and unmatchable graduation of sorts, but also a maturing and understanding and love for this treasured land, Florida. We are fortunate that this Blue Cypress Lake is protected under a strict State Conservation Program. Nothing can be removed from or even touched in this lake, not even a piece of long-dead driftwood. Only the fish may be caught by a licensed fisherman

I had to stop, place the paddle crosswise on the foredeck before me, and try to take this all in, consider how this place, the look of it, the feel, the reality provided such a grand ending to my voyage, but more, how my Florida's natural places are so significant to our very existence. It is the likes of all the Blue Cypress Lakes, all the St. Johns Rivers, all the places like that, that can bring such peace and joy to living, and how expensive losing such gems would be. All things in Florida are interrelated, interdependent. There is no way to drop one stitch in the fabric and ignore it, just carry on.

I looked back on this trip of mine, and I saw what would cause the future of my home. What we do with what we have would determine what we will become and who we are.

I picked up my paddle again and crossed the lake southwesterly to Middleton's, dead ahead. It was the only suggestion of commercialism on the lake. It appeared the early folks there wanted to keep it all a secret. It could be gotten to by boat, but there are no roads anywhere near except one, a two-lane gravel washboard that leads to Middleton's Fish Camp.

On any other day, discovering Blue Cypress Lake at the headwaters of the St. Johns River, would have been fodder enough for celebration, a grandé finalé with crescendo to remember. That day could have ended in pure joy, but, it seemed, it wouldn't.

I beached on their little ramp and walked up to their office/store's open front door. American flags out front on each side flapped in the light breeze. I needed to arrange secure storage for my kayak and gear and ask about transportation.

There was a father and son arranging for rental of a small outboard fishing rig with the young clerk at the front counter. They finished up, gathered their spinning rods, tackle box, and big cooler and left full of excitement.

I remember smiling to myself as they left. The rest of today became vague, impossible to remember with any clarity.

Everything changed. It was unavoidable.

My eyes caught the pile of newspapers on the counter. The headline, two lines of two-inch-tall-sized words above a third line, a giant, six-inch-tall single word with space between each letter, took up the whole front page above the fold line.

The clerk asked, "Now, how may I help you, sir?"

I heard his voice, but it was like a distant echo.

"Sir?"

The headline slowly burned past my eyes and into my head. I slowly grasped it:

ST. JOHNS AIRBOAT
THIEF AND KIDNAPPER
C A U G H T

I looked up at the clerk, but he had no face.
"Are you all right, Sir?"
It rang in my head like a gong, *Joleen!*

CHAPTER FOURTEEN

"Whoa." *This is Paradise, this Vero Beach.*

Clad in her tiny black bikini, Joleen's body glistened, slathered head to foot with sunscreen. She reclined flat on her back on a full-length, folding beach chair. She was lightly tanned from all her running and sunbathing during her stay at the Lone Cabbage. Head back, her well-brushed auburn hair fell just past the base of her neck. A large, ivory-colored beach umbrella was open next to her. She specifically asked the hotel beach attendant to reset the umbrella so as not to put her in the shade. She wanted the sun.

Some dozen such umbrellas, their canopies all uniformly the hotel's solid ivory color, were equal distance apart, set back from the surf, each showing the hotel's "VB" logo in a cursive style, signaling property of Kimpton's Vero Beach Hotel & Spa.

Her choice of this hotel would normally be a touch above her budget. At best, she'd be at the Holiday Inn, a block south, but this time everything was different. Things were vastly improved.

She checked in that morning, quickly changed, and rushed out to the beach. She'd been dreaming of just this. It would be her very own celebration of the new, relaxed her, calm, chilled-out, and well-deserved.

She felt proud of her accomplishments.

She landed her new gig, Friday and Saturday nights, dinner till ten, at the Riverside Café, just blocks west, right on the Indian River. It should be about the same set-up and crowd as The Lone Cabbage on the St. Johns. It would be nice and very helpful to continue to be employed. The Lone Cabbage paid her in full for her recent, though abbreviated, gig, after all the trouble she caused. Even better, they offered a new contract for up to ninety days starting October first. *Thank you, Harvey*. To top it all off, she could hardly believe it, a bonus. Manager, now beautiful new friend, mentor, and number-one fan, Harvey Streetman, said he just showed the recent accounting totals to the owners. Daily grosses were at record-setting levels. Not one single day of her appearances grossed less than the preceding day. He said, "I didn't have to remind the brass, all the advertising to promote her was deductible."

The best and biggest blessing of all, Ricky had been taken into custody. She was confident he wouldn't be bothering her. He'd been jailed and was out on bail. His parents paid. He'd be watched and wouldn't step out of line. Counsel suggested that prosecutors would know every detail about him and might elect to throw the book at him. He would likely blame her. His parents could blame her, threaten her and call her slut, whore, gold digger, and extortionist. Living out there on Jupiter Island, they had the means to ruin her.

If he got off easy, he might leave her alone and move on. She made it clear there was nothing between them when he kidnapped her.

She wasn't on this beach to worry about any of that.

He was off the streets. That's what counted. That's what made her calm, able to relax, and sleep at night. It was a new deal, recoup, regroup, and relax time.

She leaned forward to stretch and check out the beach scene. Besides the hotel umbrellas, there were others strung all along the beach, and tents, and wind shields. Lots of people, elderly, young, couples, girls and guys were basking, sun worshippers. There were children with water wings and inflatables and kids digging treasure and building castles in the sand. Some were in the water.

There weren't many beach walkers though.

Well, there was just the one at the moment, a guy, way-away, looking tiny so far south, loping his way up the surf line. Occasionally, he studied a group, as if looking for somebody, then, no recognition, a quick wave, maybe apologizing for interrupting, a "Hi, oh, sorry" gesture.

She loved doing what he was doing. She planned to run on this beach in the morning.

The day was warm. She underestimated the Florida sun in early summer, not temp or humidity, she was used to that, but the rays and the UV. She sat up and turned, looking back toward the hotel, and gave a quick hand and arm wag to attract the attention of the beach attendant.

He spotted her immediately and nodded. He hustled over, smiling, pointing at her umbrella canopy, gestured to ask if she wanted it switched to block the sun. She nodded and mouthed "Thank you". He laughed, fixed it, saluted and ran off.

The shade felt much better, delightful in fact. Just being out of the direct sun, she felt the light southeasterly breeze slip past, warm but pleasant and refreshing. The breeze carried wispy threads of salt spray that felt good on her nose, like it could clear sinuses. It made her want to breathe in deep. It carried that sea smell, fish and plankton, faintly sour, and light citrusy.

The afternoon ocean surf, more or less deserted, looked gentle and quiet. She leaned forward to watch. At the waterline, little folds of liquid silver curled over one another and slid back on the smooth wet sand. It was like watching liquid poetry. She could almost hear the lyrics, and they brought a grin to her lips.

Gazing out, she saw the distant ocean horizon was a long flat line, so far away. Close by, tiny shore birds gathered. The sandpiper had beady eyes and black stick legs. They danced, darted this way, then back that way, poking at every dying bubble, as the water slid back out across the sand. So organized, they were independent, not big but strong, doing their thing, getting the job done. It was admirable.

She'd been staring into the breeze. It caused her to blink. The salt air made her eyes heavy, on the edge of closing.

She eased back down against the long beach chair. As if giving in to nap time, she placed her dark, sunbathing pods over her eyes. Such peace could not have been more welcome. She could easily let herself slip into semiconscious slumber. Her self-induced twilight flickered through her eye pods like moonlit waves.

She dozed.

In some dark quiet channel, in a distant corner of her dwindling consciousness, a sketchy sound registered: she thought she heard her name called out, softly, like an echo.

"Joleen?"

Then it was gone.

It came again louder.

"Joleen."

Somebody was touching her shoulder.

"Joleen!"

She grabbed the pods from her eyes and stared at the wide-smiling face, the very same tan, calm, honest face she found so beguiling the day they met.

"Clayt! Is it really you?"

CHAPTER FIFTEEN

Midday, they could plainly see what was going on, but didn't.

The sun was overhead, and temperature and humidity topped out. Many of the diehard beachgoers, especially with children, were calling it a day. Tents fell, umbrellas cranked and closed, ice cubes were hoisted and dumped, and cooler lids slammed. Kids moaned and adults, hot and tired, shouted this and that. They all moved toward the parking lots.

Joleen and Clayt had to at least hear, but they reacted to none of it.

For what took only seconds but seemed hours, they just looked at each other.

"Heavens! Well, I guess you completed the entire St. Johns by kayak?"

Joleen made room for Clayt to sit on the long end of the hotel's beach chair. She swung her legs, still shiny with sunscreen, off the chair, so he could sit on the end where her feet had been.

He looked down at the space she made for him, nodded, and sat.

She slowly shook her head. "Clayt, whatever made you think I'd be here?" Her voice was soft, filled with question. "What in the world made you think...?"

He opened his hands to suggest there was no mystery involved. "Well, the kayak trip ended at Blue Cypress Lake. Wait until you see it. It's like the day it was born, like Florida's real beginning. There's a word for it...."

She said, "Primordial."

That was it.

"At the fish camp, Middleton's – it's not all that far from here—I got a lift to town, hunted up a rental SUV, went back, loaded up the kayak, not about to leave my stuff, and came back."

She thought he looked a bit flummoxed but ignored his discomfort. She found it charming. "So, you were just stumbling along the beach here? I mean... ."

He smiled and nodded as if to say, *Yes, that's about it.*

He raised his arms as if to stretch, but she knew it was a gesture of discomfort. She also knew when he lowered his arm and his hand glanced off her knee, just barely brushed it, he wanted to touch her. Her lips parted slightly at the touch, and she closed them quickly. She was pleased.

"I hadn't even checked in at the Holiday Inn Oceanside yet," he said. "I wanted to be by water, even if just for a few days. I went over to take a look at the Indian River. I saw the sign at that Riverside bar place saying you were there. You can't miss it."

She looked at him, found herself getting comfortable, let her eyes rest on his, and nodded, as if to say, *Of course, The Riverside Café.*

"I thought Joleen isn't going to stay in some dump, probably likes the sun, likes the beach, lays out on the beach, so start with the beach. I went from one end, parallel to the Ocean Drive, and worked my way up."

"And so you found me here. Incredible."

"Yeah." He didn't add that he was determined. "Also, when I was checking out at Blue Cypress, at Middleton's Fish Camp office, I saw the headline in the newspaper about the airboat being found. I just had a feeling."

"Had what feeling?"

"That I wanted, that I should… find you."

They looked at each other for seconds that no one was counting.

They let their eyes widen to the surroundings. They were pretty much alone, and the beach was nearly deserted. The sun was soon to lose its glare, begin the slow arc west, to slide off the beach, high over the hotel roof, finally to touch, then slip, behind the tall trees on the mainland.

Dusk was next.

Someone had to say something. Joleen said, "I love the late-afternoon glow on the beach, don't you, Clayt?"

He was slow to answer.

She waited, then said, "I'm glad you found me."

The words, "glad you found me," caused him to search her hazel eyes.

She looked back at him calmly.

Her eyes reminded him of a deep, clear spring, *no glamorous starlet appeasing another goof-ball fan, no. Aloof but cordial to one more sodden admirer? No. She's real. She's really real.*

"Would you like to grab a bite later? You hungry?"

"I'd like that. And you can help me celebrate."

"Celebrate what?"

"My new gig. Plus Lone Cabbage paid. Can you imagine? They offered a return gig this fall."

"That's great, but what about all that trouble, the airboat thing, that boyfriend?" He saw the flickering of several emotions, as her head gently turned side-to-side.

"It's all OK."

His head dropped. He was uncertain he understood what she meant but could see her sitting up straighter, as if to change the subject.

"Let's go to the Ocean Grill. It's so good. We can get a table or eat at the bar, whichever is cheaper. They've got great burgers, shrimp cocktail with huge shrimp, runny, lemony, spicy dip, lots of lemon slices.... I'd really like you to be my guest."

"I would love to help you celebrate, Joleen, but it'll be my treat." Beyond her words and insistence for it to be her treat, it was her fervor that made her so delightful and irresistible.

He smiled at her.

They agreed to go back to their hotels, clean up, change, and meet in front of the restaurant in an hour.

"There's an old tree trunk made into a bench in front if you get there first. The bar, built out over the beach dune, has stools right up against the all-glass wall facing the ocean. They even have water and windshield wipers on the glass to wash the salt off, so people get a clear view. You'll love just watching the water, Clayt."

CHAPTER SIXTEEN

I would not leave leave Joleen waiting for me on a log bench in front of anywhere, certainly not this Ocean Grill; she might just reconsider what she was doing with this guy from Welaka, Florida. I couldn't believe what I had to accomplish to get there on time.

When we each packed up to leave the beach, I hustled south along the surf, retracing the way I came earlier, cut up the dune bridge, and checked in at the Holiday Inn, which, I was glad to see still had the reservation I made yesterday.

The Holiday Inn front desk clerks noted the SUV parked under the entrance marquee with the bright-red kayak on the roof. I promptly told them I had just kayaked the length of the St. Johns all the way to their Blue Cypress Lake, which brought "oohs" and "aahs," but was apparently insufficient to grant me celebrity status or a discount.

I hit the hotel self-laundry room, threw everything from the duffels, including the duffels, into the washer, waited, hauled it all out to the dryer, and waited. I ran up to my room with arms full, dumped it all on the bed, breathed in the air-conditioned air, and caught my breath.

I showered, shaved, folded the clothes, flopped on the bed, and looked at my watch. I had ten minutes.

She was waiting next to the log bench. I stopped, froze in place, and stared. She hadn't seen me. Her skin was golden bronze from beach time. Her auburn hair, sun kissed with highlights, looked shorter, and was in what the girls call a layered bob look, a loose, sweeping bang to the side of her forehead. She wore a beachy, white, off-the-shoulder dress, ribbed, narrow-waisted skirt and gold-strap sandals.

She held up her hand and mouthed, "*Hey.*"

I couldn't wait to be next to her. I nearly hopped and skipped like a kid the few yards. I extended my arm, bent at the elbow for her to take, which she did.

She observed my freshly laundered khaki Bermudas and out-of-the-cleaner's shirt, white, short-sleeved, button-down and said, nodding approval, "Why, you clean-up well. Shall we?"

There were still empty bar stools overlooking the ocean. The Ocean Grill had casually placed, huge, old, bronze ship's bells, black wrought-iron gates, some to nowhere, mounted on walls. The ceramic tiles from European and Miami estates inlaid on these walls here and there mesmerized me. The dark driftwood and pecky cypress everywhere, framed pictures of famous patrons, and scenes of early days of the area were all worthy of study. The Ocean Grill was a museum, a living history of this part of Florida. The whole structure hung precariously out over the ocean dune.

The bartender stood smiling in front of us.

I said, "I'll have a glass of draft Stella Artois," and turned to Joleen.

"The house red wine?"

He suggested, "We have a nice Cabernet Sauvignon."

She nodded and smiled at me, delighted that I was delighted. "Don't you just love it?"

I pointed out over the ocean to something in the water about a quarter mile off shore. It looked like the tip of a rock with a U.S. flag flying high on a pole.

Behind me, I heard the bartender tapping something on the bar top. I turned around.

He was holding a picture frame to show me. He said, "The local scuba divers named it 'The Boiler Wreck.' Here's the story." He handed it to me, pointing at the framed picture of a ship next to the written story, which he recounted.

"She was a 300-foot British cargo ship, the Breconshire, en route from Europe to New York, diverted to Tampa to pick up cargo. She ran aground on our near-shore reefs, in 1894. Tore the bottom out of her. Sank in the shallows. All hands survived and manned the lifeboats and came ashore right where you're sitting. All that's left is the boiler. The local scuba divers, snorkelers, put the flag there to mark the location, because it's slowly corroding away."

I thought it was cool they had the whole story, framed, a picture, ready for every tourist who turned to look out over the ocean.

Joleen was pleased that I was enthusiastic. "I knew you'd spot that right away." She turned to the bartender, "He's a big-time kayaker, just finished paddling the entire St. Johns River single handed."

The bartender nodded, said, quite matter-of-factly, "This round's on the Ocean Grill." He rang the big bell hanging over the bar a single time, meaning free round for all. Cheers rang out.

I turned to Joleen, "I'm going to love it here."

I couldn't stop looking at her; she looked so beautiful. She looked back at me, probably reading the obvious. I was trying to act like I was just having a jolly-good time, and I was, totally, but I just couldn't conceal my concern. *This incredible creature's been kidnapped for God's sake.* He was still out there somewhere. My chin drooped at the thought.

"Clayt?" She cocked her head to the side.

"I got to ask you something, Joleen. If you don't feel like answering it, just say so, OK?"

"Go on."

"That pseudo boyfriend, that guy who all but grabbed you right off the bandstand at the Lone Cabbage, waiting his court date, aren't you concerned, worried about him out on bail, that he might try something again? He seems very menacing to me."

"No."

"But...."

"No. He won't risk violating bail. Not now. My worry is if the court merely slaps his wrist, a fine, maybe probation, maybe both, but nothing heavy, no jail time. That has me constantly worried."

"But he did it, Joleen."

"I think even the prosecutors, though they act serious, really think this whole thing is just another lover's quarrel. Airboat's been returned. Restaurant's probable civil case most likely quickly settled out of court, his parent's more than willing to leap at the chance to pay for the restaurant's losses, any damage to business, loss of reputation. Deep pockets talk, Clayt."

"Are you saying there are bribes in play here, Joleen?"

"Clayt, I don't know. I just think through what might be in the minds of his parents and him, depending on how the case goes. I do try, though, to keep it from my conscious mind, especially when I'm enjoying myself so thoroughly." She gave me a little smile.

I stared at the bar top, my hand on the bar next to my glass.

She placed her hand over mine and pushed it gently down onto the bar, squeezing lightly. "I want to hear about you."

"I'm just thinking about you walking back from your gig at Riverside late at night."

"I'll drive."

"Your hotel has a big parking lot. It's dark."

"I'll park by the room. Clayt, my Lone Cabbage manager-friend, Harvey, knows your dad. You were born and raised in Welaka?"

I gave up trying to outsmart Joleen.

"Well, I grew up in a little cracker house right on the point near Welaka where the Ocklawaha meets the St. Johns. Mom was, still is, a homemaker, former teacher. Spoiled me. Doted on me. Great cook. Dad, when I was little, very successful in citrus management, lots of business, had a big sailboat over on the Coast. 'Ocean Dancer' was her name, a fifty-foot ketch, taught me sailing, loved hunting and fishing from the kayak, took me with him, taught me. I graduated from UF, a major in agriculture administration. Can't dance or sing."

Joleen laughed softly. "Tell me about your dad teaching you to sail, Clayt."

"You really want to hear about that?"

"Harvey Streetman said he's a terrific guy, great sportsman, terrific sailor."

"That's true. An amazing experience. Sailing at night, he would first put me flat on my back up on the foredeck looking up into the huge balloon spinnaker sail that hung way out in front of the boat. He'd put little light strings attached on each end of the bottom of the sail, called the 'clew,' so it would be easier to feel what the sail was threatening to do, and tell me to keep that huge sail full. He taught me to watch and listen to the sail trying to fold, to feel the balance, adjust those clews with the strings. In the dark, you can't see. It becomes automatic, a touch.

"Then he put me back in the cockpit in the dark at the helm station where I was to grasp the big, stainless-steel steering wheel as if I was Captain. He'd sit close behind me, his mouth right next to my ear, the sails all perfectly set and pulling well, and he'd whisper in my ear to come up or fall off. He'd utter, 'Just a touch.' It means turn the wheel a tiny bit, one way or the other, which turns the 'rudder'. It's a paddle that's under water right under the cockpit, which turns the boat, to vary the boat's heading, take control of the boat's balance, its performance and speed. With the sails perfectly set, the Captain can simply sail his way out of a slight disturbance or temporary wind shift. He'd say, 'Just a point or two, that's all.' I could watch each point change on the big brightly lit compass right in front of us and feel the boat knife forward with power."

Joleen's eyes were wide, fully engaged on me and the story.

"He told me airline pilots usually love to sail. Many own big sailboats, just like his, because sailing is more fun than flying, though it is, in fact, the same thing. Flying an airplane is to fly through air, all the same density. But sailing is through at least two separate densities, air and water, and water is very dense."

I looked at Joleen to make sure this was interesting, and her eyes, intelligent, curious, penetrated mine, wanting more story.

"He said that's why a sailboat's 'wings,' the sails in the wind and the sailboat's undercarriage, a large, heavy, usually bronze fin deep in the water, are different looking than airplane wings. The underwater fin, called the 'keel,' goes through water. The sails go through air. He said, airline pilots say it's like rolling an airplane on its side, upper wing in the air, lower one in the drink, twice the fun. They love flying and sailing.

"He would have me go below, way up forward, in the bow peak, and put my ear against the wall. When the helmsman is in the 'slot,' meaning has the boat in perfect balance, like a pane of glass gliding without friction through the water; you will hear nothing. But if the rudder and sails are not perfectly balanced, you will hear and feel the boat throbbing, like that pane of glass, but now pushing against the water. Friction kills the boat speed. It was like magic, feeling it happen."

"That's beautiful, Clayt. Just beautiful."

"Yeah."

"In my world of music, they would call that 'dolce legato,' sweet and smoothly."

"Very nice. Tell me, how did you become a singer?"

"Wait. I want to know all that he taught you, and how you came to be so knowledgeable about Florida and the past."

"OK, but this is it. Then, it's your turn. Dad would take me a hundred yards along a stony path away from the house down to the point where the Ocklawaha River mouth joins the St. Johns. He would set me on an old, big, flat, pecky cypress stump, what he called his Think Place. That old stump was eight feet in diameter, the grain he called the color of fine whiskey. He said it stood more than a hundred and fifty feet tall when the lumber barons began the relentless quest to 'civilize' Florida. They'd what was called, 'girdle' the base of the trees first, a year before they cut them down, cutting a notch all the way around to bleed the sap, so the logs would float once cut and dumped in the river. The scalping of these cypress giants was profitable. Their milled boards sold to build thousands of mansions. The old cypress tree, his Think Place, could have been a thousand years old the day the two-man cross saws came, like thousands more along the Ocklawaha. I would sit with my legs dangling over those cypress knees and wonder how anybody could commit such a crime."

"My goodness, Clayt! Those were powerful lessons and had to make a huge impression!"

"Yes. I'll never forget them. Made a huge impression. So did my kayak trip. Now, tell me about you?"

The bartender was standing in front of us again. "The kitchen closes soon, so if you planned to order food, now's the time."

I said, "Thanks, and yes, we'll take another look at the bar menu and order." I looked at Joleen. "Another round?

"Once more, and we'll order."

"Now. You grew up in South Carolina, is that right?"

"Yes, the town of Anderson, southwest of Greenville. I went through school there, was always singing as a little girl. Mom, once, when I had a sore throat, sent me to an ear-nose-and-throat guy, who treated me and told my mom I had good vocal cords, and my oral structure was built to make sounds resonate well. That's why my tones can have that throaty, whispery-but-strong feel when I want them to. He said I should take singing lessons. We learn control when we take voice training."

"Fascinating."

"It really is, Clayt. I went to Furman University and was a voice major. I landed a few gigs around the area, sang on some radio shows. Then, I got accepted by New York's Cameron Richardson-Eames. He's a famous tenor, a Juilliard grad, who performs at Lincoln Center, Carnegie Hall. He is a recording artist. Studying with him is where I developed my style. After I left him, I did some shows in Greensville and soon after, moved down here."

We had both revealed a lot about ourselves, which felt good. I understood the discipline of her controlling sound waves, as they passed through her throat, nose, and mouth. She listened intently, as I described the discipline of controlling a sailboat, as it passed through air and water like glass. I wanted to tell her more about moving through water and know much more about sound waves moving through her, but we were hungry, and the kitchen was closing soon. We had to order.

When the waitress delivered our orders to the bar, I couldn't believe what they could do with a plain hamburger. It must have been tenderloin. Joleen had shrimp cocktail, and the shrimp seemed the size of bananas. We shared their unbelievable onion rings, a "Molehill,", their medium-sized version.

We agreed I would walk Joleen back to the hotel. I suggested the beach route to take advantage of the glorious, balmy, summer night, stars by the billions, the huge, wide silver moonbeam from a very close moon panning us, as we picked our way. The tide was out. Tiny silver bracelets rolled in, curled up, the only surf, and faded back as silvery, foil sheets, disappearing in the dark, wet sand.

We held hands from time to time, but without words the whole way, even up the dune bridge and through the muffled hotel chatter and past the music, even up to reaching her floor, looking down three stories, west over Ocean Drive from her exterior, open-air, railed corridor.

She put the keycard in the slot at her door and looked up at me, as the deadbolt clicked. I studied her eyes. There were still no words. There were just two hearts beating too hard and trembling lips and the silent song of the long kiss.

CHAPTER SEVENTEEN

For breakfast, we hustled a short distance south of the hotels on Ocean Drive to a spot called The Lemon Tree. Locals touted it as the "homiest, best breakfast on the beach." The menu was American style with breakfast all day, but breakfast and lunch only. It was crowded. There were booths down both sides of the store-front layout with a quiet, turquoise and white décor, but no blaring, bright lighting. It was comfortable, fast, good service, and a very helpful staff, so we soon got a booth.

Joleen stepped outside to get away from the noise and was talking on her phone to her trio in Orlando. They were expected by afternoon for rehearsal, on stage at Riverside Café that evening. Friday night was forecast to be clear and balmy with a moon bright over the dark, reflections-flickering, Indian River.

I needed to talk to Joleen before that night. I wanted to for some time but couldn't figure out a way that wouldn't freak her out when she stepped up to that mic and looked out over a jazzed-up crowd of glistening, expectant faces. If I showed up, and there was no chance I wouldn't, I was sure she would not see things quite the way I did. She currently chooses to "accentuate the positive, eliminate the negative."

I like to see with eyes wide open. Worried about stepping on a water moccasin? Check the water and the trees. Red eyes and snout only, all else submerged? It's a 'gator. Roaring and invisible, that's an airboat. Sometimes real seems more like nightmare. Little girls lost, like Maya Muñoz, being where they should never be? Tell me, there are people ten deep all the way around the bar at the town's only waterfront joint, Riverside Café, and there's not one drugged-up, drunk, spoiled punk in the crowd who's never heard "No" in his life?

Sorry, I don't buy it.

I wanted to tell her I thought I should be incognito, as I milled around in that crowd. I couldn't allow myself to be Joleen Jackson's body guard. I may end up guarding her body with my life, but I didn't want the label after yesterday. She was a dream come true. This is now, today.

This shouldn't wait, but wait it has to. She was back, all smiles.

She said, "The hotel's given me what they call 'acoustical perfection,' a meeting room used for recording. We'll be rehearsing this afternoon. The trio's on the road headed here. I'm excited, Clayt, aren't you?"

Joleen nibbled one piece of my toast and one sip of coffee, nothing else, yet she was all energy, the total star-entertainer, gearing up, getting that creative, every-sense-ready, adrenaline-high, to knock 'em dead. She was tuned in, turned on, and straight, counting down the minutes.

I paid the bill, and we were off and running. At least she was.

"And what are you up to today?" she asked with her cheeriest face.

Not now, Clayt. Not now. "I'm going to put the kayak in the salty water of the Indian River and see what happens. Have a look-see." What I didn't say was *Dad called, didn't even ask me about a job, said I sounded great, happy.*

I told him I'd met a wonderful girl on my trip. I didn't mention the Lone Cabbage or what she did. I said she was beautiful, talented, from South Carolina. I just let it go at that, with no details.

He said, "Mom will be thrilled I've met a nice girl."

I thought he might have some news about business. Maybe they found a real cure for the Greening Disease, something, but no. Then he laid it on me; he wanted me to come home and talk. He said folks were suggesting I run for District Representative, Florida House, and that was just for starts, even state senate, saying folks knew I was conservation-ecology dedicated. We both were. He taught me. He said folks were getting downright worried. Florida was reaching a crossroad, land, people, water, air, name it.

I finally said I'd get back to him about driving up home. I said I'd be there, just not sure how quickly. As usual, that was that. There was no idle gabbing on the phone with Dad. I heard the disconnect "click," and he was gone; I'm left hearing an airy void.

Joleen asked, which I thought was odd, "Will I see you tonight?" She was clever. She knew I'd be there, but she could tell I was distracted.

"Yeah. I'll be the tourist-looking dude with the kayak on his back."

She looked at me funny. She knew that wasn't me talking.

I could hear it coming.

"What's going on, Clayt?"

"The place is a waterfront. They get complaints when the 'noise', as it's called, goes past ten o'clock from the early-to-bed, retired folks in the homes all the way across the river. So now, weekends, there's plainclothes police on the premises."

"How is it you know this?"

"Remember? I saw the sign there that you were starting soon? I got talking to a manager type."

"So?"

"So I think what you've been saying is, for now, at least, true; no 'unrequited lovers' as fans while bail is in play. But... I don't think it's wise to let it be obvious that you and I know each other. I want you to ignore me."

She refused to let the celebrative atmosphere be shattered. "And you'll be in a baggy suit, coat collar up, bulge on your hip, dark glasses?"

"Incognito."

"You mean I must look elsewhere in the house for my handsome knight in shining khakis, who, I hope, can't take his eyes off me, who, I pray, is assuredly mad about me, and likes, no, loves my singing , too-o-o-o?" She was not going to let anything dampen the mood.

I just stood there, mouth open, and, finally, noting her enviable relentlessness, said, tongue- in-cheek, "That would do."

We got up to leave, headed past the remaining throng for the front door.

Just outside, I grabbed her hand and stopped her and pulled her to me. I kissed her with everything I felt. She slipped her free hand to the back of my neck and pulled herself to me. Our breathing was short and fast.

I wanted to say so many things to her. I squeezed her hand hard enough to leave an imprint, my thumb on the back of her palm. She broke away and rushed off. It was rehearsal time.

"Break a leg," I thought I said loud enough, maybe not.

She turned back just for a second and acknowledged, raising a champion's fist.

***

Just about the time the trio arrived, I was headed in my SUV for the Indian River Lagoon, kayak, not on my back, but on the roof.

CHAPTER EIGHTEEN

At any other time, this picturesque scene would be quite romantic; I stood at the end of a dock that protruded out from Riverside Café into the Indian River Lagoon. The sunset was past, and the surrounding water was flat. There wasn't a breath of air, and the water surface was shiny. The night turned cool. Still, the air had that weighty, balmy, summer feeling of the tropics.

My eyes scanned the water for even a tired, old, barely discernable wake of a skiff, kayak, canoe, or inflatable, any small, quiet, low-to-the-water conveyance, the kind a killer-stalker might use. A quarter mile west, over on the mainland, the fuzzy-black shoreline was dotted with beads that sparkled as if strewn here and there. Above, the western sky, dark as asphalt, showed tiny diamonds by the billions tossed against it. There was no movement anywhere—not a ripple.

Joleen insisted that to show up there, breaching bail, was beyond highly unlikely; he wouldn't take the chance of adding sure jail time.

Odds are, he wouldn't show at all, but, oddly enough, the way I saw it, odds were just that, odds. I had no idea of his case, hurt or angry, humbled or psycho. He could be just wanting a second chance, some sort of reconciliation?

Or, he was seeking revenge.

If he was there, he may not be there to plead his case. He may be haunted, embarrassed, shifting blame to her. I could almost hear him justifying his every move: after all, she failed to appreciate the cool gallantry of his ploy, his heroic lover's gig, swiping that airboat whisking her off to the good life, the dominance with his semi-automatic rifle, brandishing it like a warning, should she dare hesitate to join him. He'd say she embarrassed him and brought shame onto his family, who were socially prominent. He'd sense she's probably laughing at him, spouting off how she flat-out ghosted him. Spoiled, he'd likely have Mother's support, with her lecturing, "The girl is wrong, a showgirl-tramp out for money."

I couldn't overlook that there may be a beard, dyed hair, maybe hair longer or shorter, or maybe glasses. I had only one shot at picking out a face I'd never seen and had to do it incognito.

The crowds were there in droves. The parking lot overflowed. I heard them on Riverside's enclosed deck, their voices muffled from behind the windscreens. This distance out on the dock, I can't be seen. One step back, and I'm swimming.

I thought how hard it would be to spot a male face, one at a time, more like one per second in the deceptive strobe light, and find those treacherous eyes that could match a onetime mug shot, or find nothing, no one. I knew Joleen wanted to keep the strobe light. She liked the special effect it produced.

I walked up the dock toward the enclosed deck. It was getting loud, and I saw through the windscreens that it was jammed with people.

I slipped inside at the north doors and through the enclosed deck, casual, no rush, incognito, but grabbing a quick glance at every face while avoiding eye contact.

I edged between bodies and nodded and skewered myself into the barroom, on the west side, opposite the bandstand, looking at the backs of heads. I passed the strobe, which was visually, might as well be audibly, clicking past face after face at a dizzying pace. My eyes clouded over; it all became a blur for a few seconds, then cleared. I wanted to rub my eyes, but afraid I would miss a face behind a beard or those mug-shot eyes under one of what must be dozens of baseball-type caps.

When she stepped into that key light's bright cone, the clinking glasses, the loud barroom chatter, as if by command, would simply cease. Her mic, held close, would nearly touch her lips. There would not be the slightest evidence of distraction or intenseness evidenced by her. She was the consummate entertainer, seemingly at home and at ease. Then she would float that airy, throaty, dreamy, glorious hypnosis that was hers only for the very first time at Riverside Café. It would, once again, roll out over the water, this time the Indian River; the sound I heard that night when I was on the St. Johns was like a siren calling me. The sound said, "This is Joleen."

It was time. She stepped from the shadows onto center stage. The room darkened to where the only light was from the constant flicker of the rotating strobe that continued across walls and faces.

I avoided letting my eyes stay on her. Her overhead key light threw a cone-like shaft of bright light down to the floor, leaving a circular pool aglow at her feet. She stood just outside the little circle with her figure lit, while her face remained dark, then she stepped forward into the light. Her face expressed Joleen's classic delight and her most practiced "genuine" smile.

A hideous thought dawned on me, like an arrow across my mind: *Am I actually looking at someone's vengeful bull's eye, the target?*

My mouth dropped open, as I may have spotted a possibility just out of the corner of my eye. I blinked quickly to clarify my vision, but I couldn't help chasing the strobe. *Have I lost him? Was it just a similarity, not for real at all? I can't find him. Did I even see him?*

"Thank you all for coming, and good evening!"

A few wise guys yelled and whistled. She gave them a polite smile.

"I'm Joleen."

Everybody clapped and tapped glasses. Bottles clinked each other.

What I saw backed away from the bar was against the south wall not ten feet from the barroom door, not twenty feet from her.

"Got to ask you all a question. Is every Vero Beach night actually this... absolutely beyond... luscious?"

The applause answered. More than a hundred "oohs" and "aahs" rolled across the room.

"I'm thrilled to be with you tonight! And in Vero Beach for the very first time!"

This applause started a small stampede, seated and standing alike.

I lost him in the maze of faces, if it was him. I stood in a mob, but I couldn't see them. They were right next to me. *Did the one I saw dart toward her?* She was stunning in heels, a black, sequined sheath, her hair in that loose bob, a fiery auburn under the key light; she was the essence of poise and total confidence. She wouldn't even blink if Ricky Wentworth descended upon her dressed like the devil himself.

I still scanned that south wall near the door. The strobe caught up to where I was looking and scattered the faces.

I must get closer.

I bulled my way around the west side toward the barroom door area.

"This first song, recorded just last year by Celine Dion and Barbra Streisand as a duet, is called, 'Tell Him.' Not a bad idea on a beautiful night like tonight."

The trio brought out the strings, violin and cello, plus keyboard for the intro.

She caressed the mic with two hands.

Where is he? Maybe he ducked down, as the light passed him. He could jump on the stage just as she starts.

"I've been there, with my heart out in my hand but what you must understand you can't let the chance to love him pass you by...

"Tell him, tell him that the sun and moon rise in his eyes... and whisper... tender words so soft and sweet hold him close to feel his heart beat...

"Love will be the gift you give yourself..."

Silence tried to fill the void, as the last notes faded.

Applause, first clumsy then smattering, broke out. The roars started, as the seated stood.

This would be the time for him to make his move.

I catch myself trying to match the rhythm of that song with the clockwise turning of the strobe, as it highlights every face. It is that last lyric line, "love will be the gift you give yourself." It's that line that sticks. It seems impossible that there's a sick, full-grown little boy, who hasn't the slightest knowledge of love, here among us. Where are you?

Every head and torso is frozen in awe, only hands keep slapping hands, except one, a blur. The blur frantically pushed open the barroom double doors and was gone.

I elected not to crash across the mob right in front of the bandstand, possibly causing Joleen to freeze, freak out, or worse. Instead, I casually went around to the main dining room door.

Only a few waiters and waitresses were scattered around the room. They all listened to a lower volume Joleen on the muted speakers. I cut between tables to the foyer and blasted out the front door.

Right in front of me, not twenty feet ahead, stopped, facing outbound on the parking lot exit lane were red taillights. It was a shiny, black Porsche convertible. It said, '911 Carrera 4S Cabriolet' below the trunk lid. I looked at nearly $200,000 new! Driver's side and passenger side windows were open.

Not trusting or comprehending the scene, I inched forward and ducked my head to see in through the passenger side. A young man, in apparent pain, hunched over forward. His forehead rested against the steering wheel.

I didn't know what to say. "May I help you, Sir?" I asked.

His distorted face looked over to me. It was a perfect match. It was Ricky Wentworth.

"Just get control of yourself. Drive home, don't speed, and don't get stopped, straight to

Jupiter Island. Go on. This never happened. You were never here."

He slowly turned his head to look at me. "You, you're Clayton McIver."

I had no idea how he knew.

CHAPTER NINETEEN

I was flat on my back on the bed. My thoughts raced. Still in my clothes, I was exhausted, as I stared at my motel room ceiling even before the ten o'clock noise curfew at Riverside Café ended Joleen's performance for the night. She and her car would be happily escorted home to her hotel by her trio; they knew they hitched themselves to a rising star, so top gigs were on the horizon, TV appearances, press, recordings coming, even albums, and tours.

Earlier, I saw Joleen preparing her voice, mind, and soul for the performance. I told her I'd see her tomorrow. I didn't want to jinx anything about this big moment for her or let my presence interfere with her preparations for that night.

I was definitely at the performance and wouldn't have missed it. She may have wanted to see me there. What was her remark, "... my knight in shining khakis?" but I was drifting through the crowd. She saw me only briefly here and there. I wanted nothing to distract her in any way.

She mesmerized them.

Joleen, from what I observed, couldn't possibly have noticed any commotion during her performance. There wasn't any. She had been totally at ease throughout. For her, the night came and went without disturbance just as she said it would. She chose to "accentuate the positive and eliminate the negative," satisfied that I finally agreed with her. The huge crowd and ovations surely created a guaranteed perfect afterglow. Joleen would sense by the Vero Beach crowd her star was starting to shine. There was no point in shattering that illusion. She had no way of seeing things the way I did. *Today is not mañana.*

Hard to believe, two hours staring past that strobe at faces; they all started to look like the nighttime unadorned mannequins along Ocean Drive. It was exhausting. I never sat down. The muscles in my legs clenched, my back rigid, dizzying concentration, all while trying to look nonchalant.

Then there was the parking lot scene. I hoped that shiny black Porsche and its driver landed at Jupiter Island unscathed and unnoticed. He was lucky: At 10 PM sharp, the plain-clothed noise enforcers from the police department appeared on the scene bright and shiny, no longer just part of the crowd. His mug shot was out there. He could have been spotted and nabbed. Violation of bail was serious. I hoped he appreciated that I kept him out of jail.

Then there was that expression on his face as it morphed. He turned, recognized me, and actually said my name. I saw those hateful mug-shot eyes, expressionless, faceless, reptilian, like pit vipers. I've looked into such faces; they're suddenly, instinctively curled in survival mode before me in the dry grass and wet banks along the St. Johns River.

Lying there with my eyes wide open, I couldn't escape the truth: He had been there, he took the chance. I'm no love doctor and certainly no psychiatrist, but I would think it normal behavior if rejected, to tough it out and move on.

This was different. This was desperation, and desperate people do desperate things.

Ricky Wentworth never had to face the word *No* in his life. I didn't think he ever loved anyone and didn't love Joleen. He didn't know what love was. To him, it was possessing things. One orders and receives, or one orders and simply takes. He wanted to possess a coming starlet, like a shiny, new Carrera 4S Cabriolet Porsche. He was in that "take" mode.

He knew my name. How could he? It was obvious. He tailed us constantly since Joleen and I first reconnected on the beach just days earlier. He could've asked the Ocean Grill bartender; Joleen introduced me loud and clear. "He just kayaked the whole St. Johns by himself." The bartender rang the "free-drinks" bell. He could have seen my kayak on my rental car parked under the marquee in front of the Holiday Inn and played the "fellow enthusiastic kayaker" with the desk clerk.

He knew my name.

I was in the way.

That's why I was wide awake, staring at the ceiling. My guess, he would actually try to kill me.

***

It was dawn on Sunday morning. I didn't think I slept more than an hour total.

I decided to pay up what I owed on the rental car and keep it at least another week, but I should definitely check out of the motel. When I get back, I'll find an apartment. The beach was too expensive for an unemployed country boy.

I'd call Joleen around nine o'clock. She'll be up and running by then, having slept like a rock and ready to go get 'em. Hopefully she'd say yes, like it was a welcome distraction, when I invited her to join me heading north to Welaka and Dad.

With all this killer type stuff, was I dreaming? Was I right?

CHAPTER TWENTY

I was beyond pleased when I invited Joleen to join me on the trip north to Welaka, and she not only agreed but said she'd be delighted and literally sang into the phone, "Oh, yes! Fun!" She added, more calmly, that it will be a nice break away from hotel rooms. She said she'd never had time to see the real Florida, the back country, as she called it, and said she looked forward to meeting my family. She especially wanted to meet Dad. She said he must have been a great influence on me and wanted to see what he was like.

***

We were well on our way on I-95, just south of SR 520. I stated earlier that I wanted to turn in my rental SUV when we got back and try to buy some used piece of transportation.

Without hesitation, Joleen immediately said, "Let's take my car." It was a nice metallic silver Lexus she leased when moving to Florida. Eyes straight ahead and both hands on the wheel, I was driving her car.

We kept the rental Kayak rack, put it on top of her car, and turned in my SUV. I loaded the Kayak, attached my little orange "Keep Clear" flag to the transom, and we were off.

We were approaching the exit for SR 520 cutoff to Orlando. It passed right by The Lone Cabbage on the St. Johns River where Joleen had her recent gig. I asked if she would like to stop and say hello, and she quickly shook her head and pointed straight up the highway.

"I want to see, feel, and enjoy the scenery."

She put her window down, and her hair flew in the breeze. She was excited, watching the passing Florida landscape and absolutely cool in white shorts and a white zip Polo, with not a touch of makeup. I couldn't wait to show her off to the folks.

I kept trying, from the very first moment we started out, to figure how, and mostly when, to bring up what kept me awake all night. It was the thought that her former would-be lover might be planning to threaten her life and mine.

I almost blurted it out when I made the mistake of commenting I hadn't slept well last night, that I had bad dreams. Maybe it was something I ate. I almost slipped and started to describe the nightmarish visions: *the telescopic sight from atop the building across from her hotel room door, aimed at my back,* or *me in the same crosshairs as I walked home on a dark deserted Ocean Drive.*

I knew it wasn't the time. It would just cause a heated car discussion that would end up an extended under-the-surface argument that would carry right through arrival and right in front of the folks. My folks had the awareness of stealth hunters, particularly Mom with those eyes that analyze, can penetrate all.

I knew I'd have to tell Joleen about my run-in with Wentworth sometime, but not then. I wanted to lay a little groundwork to prepre for what would have to come later, so I glanced over at her and simply asked, "When is the court date, Joleen?"

She pulled away from the window, and her eyes, clearly visible to me in the rearview mirror as I drove, looked at me without a single blink.

"Tomorrow."

I froze hearing the word, "tomorrow." It meant jail or freedom for that animal; he'd be caged or on the loose, and, if loose, on either Joleen's or my case.

I-95's center white lines flew by, minutes, maybe miles without my noticing. All I saw was, *it's tomorrow.*

Joleen was all eyes in every direction. She took in the passing scenery out her window, and then, out past me through my side window.

"Funny, commercial ugliness on the east side, lots of cattle, some horses, open grassland to the west."

"The what you called 'open grassland' was, until recently, groves, grapefruit and oranges. Some is leased out to ranchers for grazing cattle. Grazing cattle means pollution, animal waste, and fertilizers. Rains come, and the runoff ends up in Florida's rivers, lakes, estuaries, and the ocean. It doesn't have to be that way. One problem needn't cause another. There's a thing called Ecological Planning."

Her head slowly moved up and down. She understood and wanted to know more. "You know all this stuff, don't you?"

We were well north of Canaveral into southern Volusia County. I-95 crossed a bridge which forded a gully with a tributary of the St. Johns meandering through it. Pecky cypress trees lined the banks.

She smiled and said, "Nothing looks as beautiful and majestic as a cypress tree. Like statues honoring the real Florida."

I tried to agree but choked up, so pleased by her words.

Finally, I managed, "Remember that old Cyprus stump I told you about?"

Miles and miles passed beneath us before either of us spoke. Joleen seemed deeply affected by my remembrance as a small boy. The picture of men with their huge saws attacking thousand-year-old lords of nature left her face blanched. She remained quiet, in her own contemplation for a time. Her eyes were straight ahead. Finally, she looked at me in the rearview mirror.

I said, "He called it his 'Think Place'."

CHAPTER TWENTY-ONE

I was about fifty feet away when I first saw the huge old cypress stump Clayt described as his father's think place. As Clayt, his father, and I got close enough, I stepped up onto, and circled, this eight-feet-wide platform. Its ancient concentric growth rings, by the hundreds, maybe thousands, stared up. A kind of other-worldly feeling swept over me. "Oh my, your 'Think Place,' is overwhelming, Mr. McIver."

Clayt and his dad stood off to the side, watching me.

"It is like a natural pulpit suspended in a sanctuary, surrounded by this majestic cathedral of living cypress. This river passing is 'Ocklawaha.' The sound of the ancient word resonates in my throat. It's exactly as Clayton described it to me, and you must have shown it all to him. I think Clayt said you called the grain 'the color of fine whiskey.'"

Clayt introduced me to his mom and dad up at the house not more than a half hour earlier.

Still full of enthusiasm, he said, "This natural pulpit would be a fabulous spot for introducing a new Joleen Jackson hit song. Huh!"

"Oh, my goodness!" I said. "And the sound here!" I clapped my hands just once to listen. The sound ricocheted like the crack of a distant rifle, then echoed softly through the trees.

"Unbelievable! I could stay right here forever."

Clayt's dad added, "You may be the first real celebrity to grace this place, young lady."

"Thank you, Sir." All I could do was smile, embarrassed. "But this place honors you, Sir, and what you stand for. I couldn't be more impressed, not to mention the son you've allowed into my life. You're the star in this show in this beautiful country. I'm just starting to understand your dedication to preserving it."

"Hey, Son, this is quite a woman you've brought home. Proud of you. How 'bout 'Larry' from now on, Joleen, and shelve the 'mister?'"

Clayt's gaze snapped to his father. It appeared his father didn't offer this intimacy to very many people. Clayt's mouth silently formed the word, 'wow,' just before he glanced at his watch. "Mom will expect us back at the house for Sunday dinner, her specialty."

"Mom" was a total surprise at the very first meeting at her front door. She was not at all what I envisioned. I expected a matronly doting homebody.

Sally McIver was tallish, 5' 7"ish, mid to late '40's', early '50s', long legs, tanned, in well-tailored navy Bermuda shorts and long sleeved, navy and white horizontally striped cotton top. She whirled about her sizeable kitchen with authority and ease.

Dinner was served at a large table in the middle of the kitchen, undoubtedly the traditional center for all family activity. The whole atmosphere was just like being on a farm, which Sally explained, it was before being reclaimed as home and headquarters for a grove service operation. Sally seemed in the process of returning it to a working farm with her pigs, chickens, and goats. She said, "I'll show you my prizes later."

Clayt added, "That boar hog of hers won a prize at the Tallahassee North Florida Fair."

Sally's dinner menu was thinly sliced pink roast beef with horseradish on the side, golden brown, skillet-fried thyme and rosemary potatoes, and little broccoli florets with hollandaise sauce, plus the most tender, warmest, homemade dinner rolls possible. For dessert, there were watermelon balls and vanilla ice cream or strawberry pie and vanilla ice cream.

"Mom outdid it again," Clayt observed. Silence prevailed except for the "oohs" and "aahs," and continued, everybody decided to concentrate on the feast.

Finally, Sally skillfully lifted the silence and initiated civilized conversation. "Tell me about you, Joleen. Where's home? How did you get started in your career?"

Clayt coaxed, "That ENT Doc' story, Joleen, that story."

"Well, I was always singing as a little girl. Maybe at eight, I had a sore throat for the second day, and Mom took me to an ear-nose-and-throat specialist. He looked down my throat from every angle and kept poking around down there with a tongue depressor, nodding with what turned out to be approval. He told Mom I had 'nice vocal cords' and a 'good oral cavity' for making sound resonate. He suggested I ought to get singing lessons."

"And about the education and training, Joleen, come on."

"I grew up in Anderson, near Greenville, northwest corner of South Carolina, about an hour's drive south of the Blue Ridge Mountains. Graduated Furman University, voice major. Did local clubs, restaurants, some live radio."

"New York, Joleen, New York."

I nodded to Clayt. "Yes, I got accepted to study under famous Juilliard grad, Lincoln Center and Carnegie Hall star tenor, Cameron Richardson-Eames. He helped me learn my own 'style,' that's the special way I sing."

"Wait 'til you hear her Mom and Dad!"

"Been singing professionally ever since NY. Met Clayt rehearsing my first show in Florida, a place on the St. Johns, while he was amidst traversing the length of it, single-handedly by kayak."

"The Lone Cabbage. You heard of it, Dad?"

Larry had been all ears, but he perked up for real and sat up straighter. "Yes, my sheriff's deputy-friend, Tom, told me about the place with busy crowds."

Sally said, "Dessert?" Everybody groaned.

Larry seemed to take advantage of the pause while we reconsidered dessert. He turned serious. "Time for us to chat a bit, Clayt?"

"Ready when you are, Chief."

Just like that, the two were up, chairs pushed in, and off to sit on the wrap-around porch all the way to the back.

Sally's smile slipped into serious mode. Master of multi-tasking, she seemed not only hostess-with-the-mostess, but also, a kind of tension tranquilizer, interpreter, and apologist. "Larry has some important info for Clayt that he has to get off his chest, as you might have surmised, Joleen."

I just stood there. I wanted to join the men and hear what this smart man had to say. It had to do with Clayt. It, therefore, might well have to do with me, and, from Larry's sudden demeanor, it definitely had to be serious.

Sally suggested, "Joleen, have you ever had the pleasure of being introduced to a genuine, award-winning, 600-pound-plus boar hog?"

I was still just standing there. My eyes followed the men out to the porch, but I understood the signals. Not that I wouldn't, under normal circumstances, be welcome; it was, in my opinion, perhaps that Larry insisted on total privacy, need-to-know, only.

"Clayt'll tell you all about it on your way home, Joleen, I'm sure. Come with me now. I'll introduce you to my very own little zoo."

I got the idea that, when Lawrence McIver speaks, which wasn't all that often, it would be significant, and everybody listens. I saw him as the world's most-calm, clever, pleasant, full admiral ever. Ensconced on the big commander's chair up on the huge fly bridge commanding the entire fleet, he was definitely on watch. This was his watch.

Sally's smile elevated into a broad grin, as she held the screen door open for me. "Shall we?"

CHAPTER TWENTY-TWO

It was a typical early fall Florida night. The sun had just disappeared, but the western sky still glowed orange and, at the horizon, was a band of hot golden yellow. The few small pink clouds in the west had such sharp distinct edges they looked pasted there—indications of the falling humidity and cooling temps.

Mom insisted that, if we would not spend the night, we leave before dark. I lied and said I wasn't the least bit tired and would enjoy the drive.

I gave Mom a hug, and she squeezed me back like I was leaving to climb Mt. Everest.

I patted Dad's back and said, "Thanks for everything."

Joleen hugged Mom and kissed Dad's cheek. I think they were really impressed with Joleen.

She scarcely uttered a word after we said our good byes until we eased onto southbound I-95. She appeared lost in her own thoughts.

"I loved your mom. In awe of your father. Are you going to tell me what he said?"

I figured I couldn't put it off. "He didn't want to frighten you. Knowing you're not from here, he thinks you can't know what's going on here, and he's partially right. It's like the Chamber of Commerce wants it all kept quiet."

"What kept quiet?"

"Dad has lived here all his life, Joleen. Like I have. He's seen how it once was, and how it is now, the drinking water, the wells, the aquifer, the rivers, springs, the ocean estuaries, the ocean, the beaches. He and his group look at the pollution, septic tanks, runoff, toxic algae, loss of flora and fauna. They see concrete everywhere, the out-of-control housing and commercial development. Growth being mistaken for progress; that's how they frame it."

"They? Who? What group? Frame what?"

"They say we're on the edge of no return. It is now or never."

"I think I would agree, but who? What's this all about?"

"They call themselves the 'Double F Group.' Obscure on purpose. Logo looks like a cattle brand. It means 'Florida's Future.' Started with just a few guys, but everybody seemed to agree, and it grew. First a few from surrounding areas, then two or three, men and women from each county, Putnam, St. Johns, and Flagler.

"Then, as Dad puts it, like an underground movement, he and his founding management zeroed in on two or three prominent, activist-types, some legislators, all movers-and-shakers from all sixty-seven counties in Florida—no reps so far from Broward or Miami-Dade. No one believed it would work or declined to join."

"What do they hope to do?"

"Bring the war of public rancor against out-of-control residential and commercial development to a climax. The goal? Stop all construction. Cease all construction permitting that impacts any aspect of the Florida ecology. Yesterday, if not sooner, until control is legislated. That simple. It sounds simple, but it isn't."

"And your father wants you to play some role in this movement?"

"Oh yes. I'm the guy from Welaka, nonpolitical, only somewhat known, the guy who single-handedly kayaked the St. Johns, my one and only claim to fame. I was reminded, everybody doesn't do that, you know, at least, not all alone. The few who do it, write and publish books about it, so I'm somewhat known among folks along the river, Welaka, and maybe even a little in Vero Beach. The big kayaking store in Vero Beach has already asked me to speak before their kayak-instruction classes. I'm to let it be known, the newspapers, schools, clubs, malls, social media, that I'm available to lecture about kayaking, about my unique observations and experiences, all about my trip."

"I still don't get it."

"He called the job the 'Silent Lobbyist.' He said they're recruiting a few young people from every county, achievers, people with accomplishments who can influence public opinion and deliver the group's message, be heard and cause action in legislatures. He said they're asking celebrities, TV and movie stars, all to do the same thing, though these are all gratis, but good, free publicity. He said it was my trip, by myself, south on the St. Johns, that gave him the idea."

"And what do they expect you to do for money?"

"$45,000 annual, guaranteed, paid quarterly, plus legit expenses, housing, car...."

"Wow, Clayt."

"Dad said each pledged $250 per month. They set up a tax- free $500,000 trust."

"Sounds like there's got to be something more here, Clayt."

"I have no agenda. He said they've tried to make people aware. They are aware, but Florida has been kicked off the front page, because there's so much other stuff here going on all over the world grabbing the headlines. A conservationist can't get heard. In fact, he gets booed and can't get speaking requests or dates, can't get a platform. People mistake the word 'Growth' for gospel.

"He talked about the on-the-take-politicians, fed by paid lobbyists from big real estate, big business, and big agriculture. Foot-dragging at every governmental level. Mob-like resistance from residential and commercial development, the 'build-now-pave-now, growth-is-good' population. But they, all of them put together, are a smaller voting block than the rest of us. Growth is not progress. It can be done. That's what he said."

Joleen took all this in and smiled. "The whole thing, this whole day has been tiring, I'm sure, especially for you, driving all the way up to your mom and dad's, making sure they both met me, got to know me, and the dinner. What had to be a very tense meeting with your dad, you must be exhausted. Now there's over a two-hour drive back. How about if we pull over onto the shoulder up ahead someplace, and you let me drive?"

I lied again just like I had earlier that day, which seemed ages ago, and said, "I'm not tired. Really. I'm fine."

The traffic was heavy. It was Sunday night, and people were all going home. There were no bumper-to-bumper drivers or traffic jams. There are stretches of open highway. It was getting dark, and those misty haloed streetlights, blazing searchlight-bright, that can blind one, made of sodium vapor I think it's called. They hang down one after another, stanchion-after-stanchion flipping by. They can mesmerize. Those streetlights and the car headlights reflected bright-white off the low clouds out ahead. I stared. I squinted, but I was staring. My eyes are tired.

Joleen seemed quietly relaxed, just watching the passing scenery and the cars ahead.

The cars and trucks all looked alike to me, the same, fuzzy-white-looking blobs under all the lights. I just didn't want Joleen driving on busy I-95 in the dark.

I kept counting the broken white stripes, the white passing lines adjacent on my left, each pulsing with a beat of its own as they slid under and away. My mind wandered.

Little, sweet-faced Maya Muñoz, sex trafficking victim escapee, wandering up to me at Camp Holly. My constant questions, her answers in Spanish. I finally put her in the sheriff's patrol car bound for the Department of Children and Families. She stopped at the patrol car door, smiled that smile, and waved goodbye to me. I wondered if she ever got back home to Cartagena, Colombia?

I quietly paddled along on the St. Johns, gray smoke in the distance climbing above high ground and clustered pines. It was a campsite. I beached and walked the grassy path between high grass to where the previous night's campfire still smoldered, the young boy and girl leaning back against the pines as if gazing at one another, their dull-eyed expressions. The syringes were still in their arms! They were dead! I couldn't look!

My eyes shot up and away following the trees to the sky! I slam the back of my head against the headrest!

Joleen screams.

An eighteen-wheeler, blasting my rearview mirror with bright-white lights, air horn shrieking, hurls past in the left lane. I had drifted across the white line. Jarred awake, I yanked back, just as the huge roaring truck screeched past us.

Joleen stared at me and calmly, but forcibly, said, "First chance you get, check your rearview mirror and pull over, Clayt. I'll take it from here."

CHAPTER TWENTY-THREE

It was a beautiful, clear-sky morning on Vero Beach.

The wet-sand surf next to the ocean felt good.

I mostly slept in fits all night, thinking about my trip with Clayt to Welaka and back. I'll bear down and do my usual walking routine, first speed-walking, then slow. I remembered to set my phone to "bing" me when I hit my number, 4000 steps.

We were off.

I love it. Alternate speed-walking always seemed to clear my view of the ocean horizon and straighten out thinking; not bad on thighs and waistlines either. I try to do about a quarter mile each set, as many sets as it takes to reach my daily step count.

I wish I could walk away a few things that were bothering me. What baffled me was how broadly Clayt's father spoke about his plan that involved Clayt's traveling the state. He was to talk about his kayaking trip on the St. Johns, but couched in raising public awareness concerning the terminal dangers to Florida's ecology. He would be addressing out-of-control real estate development. It sounded innocent enough and was clever. Maybe the plan was perfectly clear to Clayt, and he just didn't want to bring up any less-attractive aspects to me yet. I could only guess.

I had questions.

It seemed to me the plan was not simple to execute. Couldn't it be dangerous? After all, the goal seemed to be to clash with and defeat "Big Power," an army of uncontrolled growth advocates, accused of destroying the state's ecological future. That was no nursery rhyme. Those weren't toy soldiers in such an army. Even in the entertainment biz, as I know well, competition is rough, and it can and does get nasty. The other side of that coin, the old quote is true "they're just not making land anymore." Some very tough people—or their paid hoods—could get very mad at the "Double Whatever Group," i.e. at Clayt. My Daddy used to say, "The more precious an idea, the more priceless the value." I wondered what "priceless" might mean in terms of Clayt's life?

Another thing on my mind was that this is sentencing day for Ricky Wentworth. When the verdict came down a week or so ago, felony third degree, I had a brief moment of hope. The picture quickly got real. There was no previous record, first offense, just a lovelorn boy-with-trust-fund who lost his cool. Momma, with her contacts galore among the higher-ups, she would be in the front row. Daddy, even if all he does is write the checks, could call-in a favor or two. My guess remained the same. He would get off scot-free, no jail time likely. There would be probation, big fine, "thank you Momma and Daddy," maybe community service, slap on the wrist, and then... back on the street. I'd just have to deal with it. I would not let it ruin my plans.

I had to stop and take a breather. I was out of breath. I needed to bend and stretch my hamstrings.

Shells were everywhere. *Oh, look, that small shell is pretty, but here's a hairline crack nearly through. This one gets slipped into my pocket. It's my "wish-for" shell, so all my future wishes come true.*

I loved watching the ocean, forceful and relentless.

My feet settled in the wet, mucky sand. The gentle surf wrapped around my ankles, flowing back out from around them, carrying with it, sand. I sank deeper. I felt as if I was without an anchor. I just hoped Ricky wasn't thinking of revenge when he thought of me.

I pulled up each foot and stepped back.

Oh, damn. Phone has to buzz now. I regained balance, touched "speaker," and waited.

"Hi, Joleen. Tom Mackey."

"I'm sorry, Tom who?"

"Mackey, Sheriff's Deputy Tom Mackey. I discussed your kidnapping with you in the office up at the Lone Cabbage?"

"Oh, yes, the deputy with his very own motorcycle." (*Wasn't he the Detective who seemed so supportive and knew what really happened? Yes.*)

"Yeah, it was our jurisdiction. I thought your position warranted credence the day I talked to you, if you recall. I gave you my card and told you to call anytime."

"Yes, I still have your card."

"Well, my boss has been asked, and has, in turn, asked me to monitor you in my off-duty time, which I've agreed to do."

"Well, Tom, that's very kind of you, but...."

"Don't worry, Joleen, I'll remain invisible. You won't even know I'm there."

"May I ask who asked your boss to have me looked after?"

"He didn't say, and I don't ask, Joleen. The point of my call is sentencing came down this morning, as you're doubtless aware. I thought you might appreciate clarification of the details."

"OK. What details, Tom?"

"Judge ordered probation, a year, must report to a probation officer, counseling, community service, plus $5,000 fine...."

"Yes. Back on the street, Tom. Right?"

"True, but with a permanent record."

"Can't Momma or Daddy get that buried?"

"I talked to Mr. Wentworth, Joleen. He said he wanted nothing to do with the whole mess. He was disgusted with his son. He wasn't once in court."

"Interesting."

"That's not all. The judge handed down a No Stalking Order. Richard Randolph Wentworth III is not to attempt to make contact with you in any way and is ordered to remain no less than 500 yards from you at all times."

"I see. So I somehow have some guarantee that I'll be safe?"

There was a pause. "We'll be watching his every move, Joleen, and I hope he turns himself around. I'll be in touch with you if I spot anything at all that concerns me. I'll let you go now, but call with any concerns you have. 'Bye, Joleen."

I heard the phone click, and he was gone. I've got to check and make sure his card was safely in my wallet and put his number on my speed dial.

CHAPTER TWENTY-FOUR

I was actually excited. I was in a car I actually owned. I must have hit every used car lot between Melbourne and Stuart. I was on the road with it heading home. I thought Joleen would like it. It was a metallic-silver, 2014 Nissan Rogue SUV with 38,000 miles. Unbelievably, I found a rental that morning from an elderly, retired couple moving north to be with family but holding onto their Vero Beach address for the present. According to the rental agreement, I had it for at least six months. It was a real stroke of luck. Walk out the door, and we're on South Beach in Vero Beach. Joleen would flip. She won't believe I found it.

That morning—got to remember this stunt—I was lecturing on my St. Johns kayaking venture to a new kayak owners' and prospective buyers' class at the Vero Beach kayak store. Forty to fifty gathered around me. I turned a Kayak just like mine upside down, showing a capsizing drill. There was a small straight back wood chair in the corner. I grabbed it, slowly turned it from right side up to upside down while I described the way to feather and swing the paddle and move my body. They loved it. I got their attention. More importantly, I got them interested in taking capsizing-up-righting lessons taught in a local swimming pool. It's absolutely necessary for the serious kayaker.

What I have to remember, though, is that when I talked about Florida's ecology being in trouble, the whole group went silent. They didn't want to talk about it, or couldn't, and maybe felt helpless, I don't know. I was talking about some aspects of camping, early planning and reconnaissance, equipment like bug netting, and situations like no running water, etcetera.

In the back of my mind, once again, were the two dead druggie kids whose campsite I'd walked up on that morning on the St. Johns. I still see that smoke rising. The meeting just went downhill from there.

My mind hashed this over.

The natural inclination among the population seemed to be that growth is good.

People really don't realize that growth isn't always progress.

The same thing happened last night at the Elks Club. I was invited to tell about my trip by a member-kayaker. I mentioned that the natural fresh-water springs in the St. Johns were pumping out far less volume, drying up, according to the Florida Department of Environmental Protection and didn't even finish saying why: lessees, and bottled water companies were sucking it up like never before. The room, probably a hundred people, went hush, silent, same as before. I can't figure out how to deliver the Double F message. People turn off when they feel helpless. I could almost hear the question behind the bewildered faces, "What can I do?"

My first thought was, I should stick to extolling Florida's natural resource virtues, unpolluted water, forest areas, green space, and contiguous wildlife corridors and habitats, and let the audience transpose the pros into cons and conservation. I could talk all day about beautiful mornings paddling through clear, moving water, feeling the early sun, leaning over to study sea life, watching, learning currents from floating plants that never touch bottom. I could describe turning your face to face the cooling rain. I could go on and on about late afternoons, stopping to admire a surrounding swamp of grass that stretches in all directions past all horizons, and nights stretched out in my tent, sleeping on billions of shells in mounds thousands of years old. These are experiences only this paradise can offer.

People are busy. They forget the adage, "they don't make land anymore," so what are we leaving for the next generation?

Criticizing growth by criticizing real-estate developers may not be the way to go. People can't face the choice: paradise or a concrete peninsula. They take the easier road, "Growth is inevitable," which is true, and that's the problem.

I neared the freeway exit to Vero Beach. The miles went by fast. Another problem I notice, passing all the open land that was, up until recently, citrus groves has become barren grasslands. It's been wiped out by the Greening Disease. Sometimes every tree in a grove is ripped out of the ground, piled up in huge ugly piles, and burned to stop this killer spread by a deadly Asian insect. Some growers have been quoted as saying they're close to being out of business. Costs are up, harvests are down, and profits are gone. They call their once-thriving citrus industry "ghost groves." One can't blame them if they look to real-estate development to try to recapture value for their land. From what I see, the developers are swooping in like vultures. Two thousand newcomers a day moving here means the pavers and builders are drooling.

I had no idea how to do what Dad asked me to do.

Joleen had an uncanny ability to read people. She automatically watched their faces when she sang to get reactions to her songs, sensed their moods, how to judge audiences, set them up, keep control of the scene. I couldn't wait to discuss this all with her.

I crossed the bridge to beachside. I told her on the phone I'd pick her up in front of the hotel. She didn't believe me about the beach condo. I said, "Just check out of the hotel. I'll pick you up at four P.M."

At five to four, I was curbside, and there she was.

Just look at her. Even with her luggage piled on the curb, even the large costume garment bag on wheels standing there, she still had that great, zillion-dollar Joleen smile. The more I looked at her, the more I wanted her with me always, the more I loved her.

"Hey, there. Your dad called. Did he call you? He wants us in Palm Beach for some meeting tomorrow. Both of us." She took a quick glance around. "Nice car." She pointed at her luggage for me to handle and slipped quickly onto the passenger's seat. "Shall we?" She was definitely ready.

Dad called, and it was never just to say hello.

CHAPTER TWENTY-FIVE

His call yesterday to meet this morning at some downtown office in West Palm Beach sounded so pressing, arduous, and painstakingly clear as to place, address, exact floor, and exact time to appear, was so unlike Dad that it baffled Clayt. Just as curious was Dad specifically requesting Joleen be with him. Why?

At crack o' dawn, he and Joleen hit I-95 South and arrived at the right location and address at exactly 10 A.M. They were in front of an ultramodern high-rise at the east end of North Clematis Street overlooking the park and Intracoastal Waterway at North Flagler Drive, apparently a very top-of-the-line address.

Entering the building, they took the elevator. It climbed soundlessly up floor after floor and finally faced an expansive, luxurious foyer with high ceilings. A wall of well-lit, clear glass from floor to ceiling formed the far side of the foyer. Clear glass doors with polished brass hinges and brass opening levers revealed a modern office reception area within. Eye level on each door was written, 'RWA INC." the company name, in shiny brass letters. Touching the brass levers opened the doors.

They were greeted by a young cheerful receptionist at a stark-white, futuristic, pedestal desk, behind which was a wall of rough mahogany squares. Dozens of variably sized framed photos of apparently famous people overlaid the mahogany. The place oozed understated success.

"Good morning. Oh, you must be Joleen! Oh, hi, I'm Trish. Love your voice. So nice to finally meet you."

Joleen, not a bit surprised, nodded, "Hey, Trish, thanks. My friend, Clayton McIver."

Trish acknowledged the intro and escorted them to a plush conference room. "The president will be with you in just minutes." She left them and closed the door behind her.

"Hi, Son." Larry McIver sat at one end of the long conference table.

"Hey, Dad, you beat us." Clayt had at first thought the room unoccupied.

Dad looked tired but at ease.

"Got here before eight," he said, without looking up. Then he spotted Joleen behind Clayt. He stood, and his smile widened. "Ah, and nice to see you, Joleen."

He nodded at the far door. "Our host is Double F Group Chief of Activities here in Palm Beach County. We had a lot to talk about regarding today, and he asked that I get here beforehand. He has a keen finger on the pulse of things, very keyed-in on trends, what's happening, politics, showbiz, name it. I've found, since getting to know him that he has longtime in-depth experience and a considerable record of success in dealing with public figures, negotiations and, say, agreements, methods of compromise, all matters of interest to us. He'll join us as soon as he finishes some personal business. Shouldn't be long."

Clayt looked at Joleen, then back at Larry. "Dad, why did you want Joleen to be here, too?"

"Oh, sure, of course. Our host's idea. Best he explains himself. In the meantime, Clayt, the Group has polled the members and come up with a prospect for you to consider. We asked every county, all sixty, to submit member names they would like to see carry our banner in the political realm this coming election. Some heard you speak at Elks Club, Rotary, biz organizations, others heard or read about you, your dedication and understanding of the Florida Ecology—a number were kayakers. You were among those picked. With your agreement, we want to enter your name in the upcoming primary election for Senate, United States Senator from Florida."

Flabbergasted, Clayt sat up straight, mouth open. "You're kidding, of course."

Joleen's fingers pressed her lips. "The actual Senate?"

They both swallowed hard.

The door opened at the far end of the conference room and in came an athletic-looking 60-to-65-year-old with flushed tan cheeks and white wavy hair. He wore a perfectly tailored, lightweight, dark-gray, pinstriped suit, bright-white button-down shirt and black tie. He sat at the head of the conference table and scanned the three faces before him.

"My great grandfather started RW Enterprises selling cigars out of a horse-drawn wagon sloshing through the ruts of what later became Gratiot Avenue in Detroit, Michigan. That, over decades, became a dozen companies under the RW Enterprises banner. I founded RW Artists, Inc., thirty-odd years ago, made myself president, built it up, helped make it successful, finally retired but kept control. I'm back in the saddle, but hopefully, just for one very special client. Our business is talent representation; we're a talent agency. As you may have noted on the reception wall, our client list represents the biggest names in their fields the world over, in entertainment, music, art, Broadway, off-Broadway, Hollywood, and working at the world's finest venues, top hotels, clubs, restaurants, charity and special events. We have one motto, 'We Make Stars.'"

He stood up straight and let his arms reach out to each side as if to request their indulgence. "My name is Rand Wentworth, perhaps more recognizably, Richard Randolph Wentworth, Jr., Ricky's father."

Larry McIver, earlier informed, sat back and watched the shock show on faces.

Clayt remained still except for clenching his jaw. Joleen's intake of breath was almost silent.

Wentworth immediately went on. "Before you both get up and march out of here, I want you to know that this whole affair has all but snuffed out the lights for me. I apologize from the bottom of my heart for what he put you through, Joleen, and you, too, Clayton. As you may be informed, I refused to appear in court. My attorneys are instructed to remove him as trustee from the family trusts. The week after official charges were presented in court, my wife requested I remove her from our home to an assisted living facility here in Palm Beach. He broke her spirit. He broke my heart. He embarrassed and destroyed what little I had as a family. I realize it was fundamentally my fault, our fault. We neglected the boy in most ways and were distracted and too busy, It's an old story, too often told. We tried to make up by opening the checkbook." Rand's head quivered almost imperceptibly. "Please forgive us, my wife and me. I will more than make recompense, I guarantee."

Joleen stared at him, slowly grasping his sincerity.

Clayt nodded slightly but with a furled brow.

"Oh, and one more thing, Joleen. Just one more minute, if you will? I always tried to judge talent by being 'on scene' at some point, not watching pictures of art being created, not listening to recorded actor's speech, not CDs, tapes or digitals of auditions, no second hand stuff. Before judgment, it had to be live, real, in the flesh. In my opinion, that depth analysis is exactly why our motto has rung true so many times beyond the odds: 'We Make Stars.'

"After you, fortunately, returned to work at that Lone Cabbage Restaurant place, after the theft and your kidnapping, I stole out of here early one evening, unknown to anybody, not even Trish, not even using the front door, out the back, so she couldn't know. I drove up there.

"It was already dark. The parking lot was jammed. I slipped in through the crowd unnoticed, stood in the semi-dark, in a mass of bodies. I stood behind the bar stools, all of those occupied, all eyes on the bandstand. One tiny key light sent a shaft of light down to the stage floor.

"What a crowd. All in the dark. All faces glued to a single circle of light. I ordered a cold, tall, Pilsner glass of draft beer just as you stepped into that key light for the last song. The sight of you on that stage that night, your beauty, your poise, the confidence, that exploding, joyous smile that said 'thank you' in a thousand languages; you mesmerized not only me but the whole house.

"Of course, you eventually had to arrive at that last lyric and that last note of the last song. The sound from that throat of yours threaded across the room like the whisper of night air through southern pines. How could such a feather float, still heard, across that restaurant's patio, rise up so gently over the St. Johns and seemingly, never quite disappear? It is surely still out there. One day soon, Joleen, it will be heard... everywhere."

CHAPTER TWENTY-SIX

Rand so dramatized his pronunciation of the word, "everywhere," it seemed to reverberate off the conference room walls. For a brief moment, all three listeners were silent, pleasantly shocked.

Larry stood and initiated a one-man round of applause.

Clayt, on the edge of his chair, joined, cheering.

Joleen struggled, making every effort to enjoy Rand's praise and the show of approval, but her jaw trembled, and finally, she looked up, blurry-eyed, but proud, and mumbled, "Clayton! Oh Clayt!" Tears flowed.

Rand bit a twitching lower lip, brought a trembling loose fist up to his mouth to clear his throat, and muttered a clumsy apology for his exuberance. An accomplished executive, he quickly tried to recover and went on as if he'd simply quoted the day's stock or dictated some note to Trish. "I have a Proposal To Represent, that's a contract by RWA for your consideration, Joleen. Two copies, one for your signature, should you elect to sign, the other for your records. You can pick them up from Trish out front, as you leave today."

Larry, rose, saying, "How 'bout that, young lady!"

Joleen looked to the ceiling, her cheeks wet, and could only mouth, "*Wow*."

Clayt was on his feet.

Larry patted the tabletop. "Well, does that about cover everything, Rand?"

Rand put up his hands to stop any move toward adjournment. "Hold on, everybody. One more thing. Meeting Joleen gave me an idea about handling Clayt's speaking engagements for the Double F Group, not to mention for what could be next, a political campaign."

Clayt sat back down.

Larry did as well. "We're all ears, Rand."

Larry was gaining more and more respect for this promotions expert, realizing Double F needed idea people like Rand. On the phone several times over the past days, discussing the upcoming meeting, and learning the man had refused to attend the court proceedings even though it was his own son charged, and his wife, disillusioned, had given up. Larry saw a different character emerging than the one he envisioned as Richard R. Wentworth. Underneath it all, the man was not only smart, but the real thing. The man had heart.

With a nod, Rand said, "Watching Joleen's performance that night, you could see how she opened. She was all smiles, offered a very feminine, graceful bow from the neck to show her appreciation to her audience. She specifically mouthed the words *"Thank you"* to the entire house. When she had the audience ready—note I said 'she had the audience ready—that's when she launched her magic. I suggest we take advantage of that mastery and have Joleen accompany Clayt as often as she can, on stage. Maybe even speaking briefly, perhaps introducing Clayt, or introducing related subjects, observations, announcing agreements reached." Feeling he'd made his point, Rand polled each face. "What say you all?"

Clayt cocked his head left, looking away from the others, questioning, fearing what he was hearing. "I've come to ask myself, about some of those larger speaking engagements to more or less full houses, after I've tried to get real about the meaning of lost green space, the lost wildlife habitat, pollution, the state's fresh-water dilemma. I lost the audience. I ask you, what is going to be their reaction if I say, 'Every aspect of Florida's ecology is inter-related. You drop one stitch, and it all comes unraveled.' What if I bring up that 'overbuilding' could eventually lead to no drinkable water, no life?' What if the audience is all pavers, brick layers, carpenters, plumbers, electricians, roofers, all wedded to 'Big Money Developers?'"

`Clayt paused, searching faces. "I still have to walk out the back door of that place in the dark afterward." He nodded for emphasis. "And now, you're talking Joleen being with me?"

He stared at his dad.

Clayt's dad rubbed his chin, head down.

Joleen's face was a grimace, biting her lip, at the thought of what might happen out that back door in the dark of night. Nevertheless, she silently, in her own mind, agreed with Rand. She could influence the conduct of an audience, even their comprehension.

Rand quietly stated, "That's why I've recommended armed protection for each of you speakers. That's why I hired Sherriff's Deputy, Captain Thomas Mackey, to tail you, Clayt, just like I've had him tail Joleen."

Joleen responded, "Yes, I remember. He said I'd never know he was there. Gave me his card to call him if, for any reason. I put it on speed-dial on my I-phone."

Rand continued, "Tom knew your father, Clayt. When I first met your father, involving Double F Group business, eventually, my concerns for Joleen came up in discussion. I had been concerned ever since Ricky was caught and arrested. I'd lost all trust. Wasn't sure what he might do. I only knew there was a Joleen Jackson onboard that airboat that night. Larry mentioned Tom, finagled a deal with Tom's boss, his friend the sheriff up there, and introduced me. Tom Mackey's a Double F Group member now. Tom's a tough cookie but clever, takes no crap, but subtle, dresses down in more ways than one. He said people don't even know he's there; he passes for a biker. He's invisible to the bad guys in that black motorcycle jacket of his. He's how I've been able to feel a little less concerned about Joleen's safety."

Joleen bit her lower lip and closed her eyes for a second. She finally got the answer to who requested Tom be assigned to look after her. She remembered asking that question of Tom, and he replied, "You don't ask." She finally knew it was Rand Wentworth, Ricky's father.

Clayt, head down as he listened, slowly looked up, staring at Joleen.

Rand continued, "Clayt, when your father first told me about his idea of making you one of our speakers and your single-handedly kayaking the entire, long, St. Johns, and learning of your ability to relate that experience, I knew. With your understanding and appreciation of our natural resources, I knew, we had the spokesman for the entire Double F Group mission."

Rand set his jaw. He looked around the table, studying faces. "In closing my remarks, just let me say, we're out of time. Florida population is exploding. New subdivisions are creeping in at an alarming rate across what were, just yesterday, citrus groves. New roads and demand for services. We are paving paradise! We're ecologically at that point of no return, this according to dedicated conservancy land trust authorities. We'll not get it back, and it will kill this paradise. It's now or die."

The following silence said, *this meeting is over.*

They all stood.

Trish handed Joleen a large manila envelope on their way out. The two exchanged smiles, and Clayt threw Trish a quick salute.

The big glass doors of RWA, INC. swung open, closed, and Joleen and Clayt were headed down the foyer. As the two waited for the elevator, Clayt thought, *One, or, more likely, both these two faces will be framed and on that mahogany wall.* He would bet on it.

"You say something, Clayt?"

"Just thinking."

The elevator doors opened.

CHAPTER TWENTY-SEVEN

Just before dawn the morning after, the two of them sat next to each other on the beach. He sat on his haunches, toes nearly in wet sand. Her knees were tucked up under her chin, held by her arms, as they waited for sunup.

The tide was out, and a thin, colorless, slippery, liquid carpet slid up, rolled over, reached their toes, and died in wrinkled silver threads sent by the crescent moon.

They stared out at where a horizon line would soon appear in the darkness, then that warming summer blue of a late August morning.

Summer was slipping away. Hurricane preparedness was already a subject on TV weather shows. Come October, dead ahead, Joleen would head back to the Lone Cabbage, on the St. Johns River, west of Cocoa Beach, for her three-month winter season. After that, it was New York for album work, her proposed new album, soon to be in negotiation with a top recording label, conducted by RWA, her new talent agency. She was ready to sign her contract and return it first thing Monday.

Yesterday's meeting was all they talked about all evening and through the night.

Clayt couldn't sleep. A new bout of insomnia was because he wasn't the least bit comfortable with "putting it to" a bunch of uneasy construction workers at some Double F Group-sponsored speaking engagement, especially with Joleen onstage with him. His distractions might seem academic to a casual observer, but their solution exactly defined the paid job he accepted from the Double F Group, and he had no idea how to do that job.

They got up, donned T-shirts and shorts, and stepped out the front door onto sand. The Condo Document's architectural drawings of their new South Beach rental displayed the back door, facing the ocean, and the front as the one off the parking lot, facing west. They laughed at that. To these two, facing the ocean was, had to be, front. They loved it and were so happy to be on the beach.

The surroundings were symbiotic with their deepening love.

Earlier, Joleen grabbed the morning Press Journal off what they called their 'back' door steps and glanced around the full brightly lit parking lot. She spotted the motorcycle right away. It had a familiar look. Oh, probably not, but she was pretending. Maybe not, but she was just twisting the truth. She wished she could wish it away, but it was more than familiar. *Ok, but I will not let this be a topic of discussion on this beach, now or any time!*

They sat on the sand as silent as mimes.

"What's gotten hold of that beautiful head of yours, Love?" She didn't want to break into his thoughts, but he hardly said a word since they got up.

"I was just thinking." He unenthusiastically threw up his arms in dismay, as if he had no more to say. "Just bothered by some of the talk yesterday." It had been a major undecided point at the big meeting in Palm Beach with Clayt's dad, Larry McIver, founder of Double F Group, and Rand Wentworth of RWA, a Double F member and charged with Palm Beach County. The undecided point and the point in contention was about Joleen and himself, as a team, involved in Double F Group political action.

On stage. Joleen saw threats. Clayt saw true danger. She thought he might be magnifying it. He thought about tough construction workers being told their way of making a living had to be curtailed... and in the back of his mind... a meeting in a dark alley with Ricky Wentworth. Did he foresee professional protection police or even Captain Thomas Mackey as a 100% guaranteed shield? It was chancy.

Joleen, back from Palm Beach, was ecstatic with her contract, but on the outside she wanted to appear casual, unaffected. She couldn't gloat while her lover was so unsettled. Her worry was Clayt, who was scheduled to speak before a builders' association meeting this week and a large condo association.

Clayt turned directly to her, finally about to talk.

Thankful, Joleen just listened.

"Every Floridian should have the opportunity to take the trip I've taken. Some three hundred miles at two or so miles an hour, single-handedly, alone, in a ten-foot kayak, on one of this peninsula's oldest rivers. It taught me the real Florida, our natural resources, not value in terms of dollars but in terms of respect. What has value somehow evades destruction.

I remember finding myself one typically clear, bright Florida morning, probably around eight AM, in the middle of huge Lake

George. That lake," Clayt gently shook his head in admiration, "is actually an ancient expansion of the St. Johns; the river simply overflowed into this shallow flood plain thousands of years ago. There's almost no lake current, but the river kept on flowing right through it."

Joleen cocked her head. This was headed somewhere.

"There was no breeze at all that morning. The lake was like a giant glass mirror in every direction as far as I could see. There was absolute silence with not another soul anywhere. In the distance to the south, a singular, huge, gray cumulonimbus thunderhead mushroomed up, miles tall, slowly sliding left to right, not quite toward me. I watched it pass me to the west, dumping misty columns of rain on the state's western grasslands, crop lands, our wildlife corridor, trees like cabbage palm, saw palmetto, buttonwoods, oaks, maples, cypress.

"The moisture that caused that rain had been sucked up out of our very own hot, Coastal Florida Atlantic waters to form that cumulonimbus. It was carried on our very own prevailing southeasterly. The big cloud had two choices, burst upward and let the water evaporate into the atmosphere or, if too heavy because of the moisture, let it pour, irrigate our crops and greenery, wash our clothes, and hydrate every living thing."

He looked at Joleen, his eyes glassed over with gathering thought. He touched her and spoke again. "I never thought about it until then. What I was watching was our aquifer magically re-filter, and recharge our state's water supply, a miracle of natural science. That was not Iowa rain blown over from Nebraska. That was all Florida, born and raised, unique to Florida.

"Another plus was that particular thunderhead missed me." Clayt laughed softly, looking into Joleen's eyes. "I got hit later by its brother. I even capsized, but that's another story."

She bit her lip, wanting more.

"A few days later, near dusk, I found myself surrounded, again, as far as the eye could see, by a huge endless swamp. Tall yellow sawgrass, golden in dying light...." He made a waving motion, looking for the right word. "...undulating like a gently rolling sea. It was so huge there were no horizons. I was looking out across, searching for the edges, the ends of what had to be a flat world. The St. Johns had hundreds of channels through the massive swamp, some miles long, but often, dead-ended. There was no such thing as penetrating those thick walls of grass. Caught in a dead end meant paddle twice the distance and gain nothing. You had to turn around and paddle back to the beginning. I had plotted my course, choosing the fastest-moving currents and backing up with GPS. I was thankful I had it aboard.

"That beautiful swamp, filtered the waters, preserved it, and sheltered baby fish and game. I watched one of God's natural miracles in action that day. It was the reality of a story I've heard all of my life—for as long as I can remember.

"At that moment I was popping my tent and spreading open my sleeping bag atop millenniums-old shell mounds." Clayt shook his head slightly, side-to-side, capturing his initial wonder that moment.

Joleen was wide-eyed.

"The wading birds and others feed on the area snails, and deposit shells right there where the snails live. They were piled up in mounds for generation upon generation until they reached above the water line as dry mounds, called shell mounds. These are places that show life is meant to go on.

"You can imagine my thoughts as I lay there on these centuries-old former living things. I said a small prayer that night."

His head dropped millimeters.

"All memories are worth more to every Floridian than all the gold on this planet."

Joleen's head rose. She looked at Clayt, as she had never before.

"Clayt, my beloved Clayt. I've never heard anything described more graciously or beautifully." She broke into a gentle smile. "I think I just heard the elegance of lyric poetry." Her eyes sparkled as she caught his eye. "That's magic, Clayt."

Clayt just smiled and bit his lower lip.

"I may be onto something. Present the value of all I saw on my journey and let that value demand preservation." He dropped his head again. "Would that, do you think, demand altering public opinion, and demand survival?"

He stood, shook the sand off his feet, and gestured toward the condo.

She hesitated, then followed. As they trudged across the sand, she remembered the sight of the motorcycle. She knew, full well, who it belonged to. Why was he here? He parked so close to their cars. Why? He said she'd never know he was around. He had a reason. That was the scary part.

Clayt stopped and turned around to look at her as if she stumbled.

CHAPTER TWENTY-EIGHT

I want to explain myself. Nobody anywhere. There's just me sitting on this small dune in the dark alone on the beach. Joleen, as well as Clayton McIver, aren't mine to toy with anymore. I know that now. They're separate from what I've wanted from them to be, what I wanted to take from them. They are their own, as they were this early dawn, sitting here side-by-side.

I'm here, always as I have been, just a mark on the surface of life, trying to grasp the bits left by others who have had the meat of life.

They were so in love, so perfect a match.

I am, I know, I've always known, a leftover person, someone who can only live through hand-me-down emotions. I fell overwhelmingly, desperately in love with an elegant, beautiful, talented goddess, but had no skills of any kind to share with her. Never have. Never been tutored in the ways of living life.

After our first date, up in North Carolina, near her home, I claimed possession, as if she were a new red wagon just given to a little boy. I don't know why I never knew I can't just take another person. This is what a rapist feels. I am no better. I am an emotional rapist. It all comes from self-pity even if I have reason to pity myself.

I was born, but not raised. I was just placed, situated. Maybe these people who conceived me forgot that. Maybe they were also situated. Maybe they didn't know the difference.

I saw a lot of nannies. Of mother, not so much. She'd put her hand under my chin and raise up my face. God, I loved that. Loved those moments. She'd say, "My dear, dear boy," but I wanted her to say it again. I'd try to get her to sit down and say it again and sit on her lap, but instead, she said it standing up, walking through the room, on her way somewhere else. One time I pulled at her long skirt—took the end of the skirt in two hands and tried to drag her to the couch, so she'd let me sit on her lap and then she'd say that, but I pulled too hard. I guess I ripped a seam in her skirt, and she got angry and shouted, "Don't pull at people, Ricky!" My first attempted rape, I guess.

When I was five, I remember I had a question welling up in me, and I remember even then knowing that it was a big question. That might have been a time I felt something of being noble, because I remember spending hours finding shreds of courage until I finally said it. I looked for my mother all over the house. I found her on her chaise lounge. I went right up to her and said, "Do you love me?" She blinked and smiled, perhaps stunned by the question.

I remember crying a lot.

Later, still a little boy, I came naked and wet out of the shower and asked my father "Do girls peepee just like I do?" He was rushing to some important engagement, that attaché case of his in hand. He said, "Look, Son, I don't have time to explain that now. Where's Loretta? Ask her, and we'll talk later." Loretta was my nanny then. We never talked later.

I went to boarding school. They said I'd no doubt make friends in life, so those friends might as well be from influential families. There was no right and wrong in my life, only degrees of, what, opportunity? I didn't even recognize the pool of self-pity my heart had crieated around me and I swam in every day, every night. I don't know why self-pity is no longer serving me, why something knocked into my head and made self-pity seem puny and false. I guess it was like a candy that disappeared the more I sucked on it, but had nothing left to give me.

Something inside shook me and told me I'm a human being, meant to cut puppet strings of early life and live like a God-damned decent person. I felt disdain for my grasp-raping ways, but I can't find the feet to stand above it, to be—noble?—yes, noble, and to state outright my deepest regret for all I've done and been.

I'd hoped to be able to say all this to them, to tell them this, to tell them I'm sorry, that it's come to me I had no right to try to steal their lives.

I have caused them both anguish and fear. I'm sorry. I'm so sorry, Joleen and Clayton. Maybe I could write it?

***

Deputy Captain Tom Mackey rang the bell at the parking lot door. Joleen answered it.

He said, "I guess you could tell I was in the area. I parked so you'd know."

"Yes.... Tom?"

"He's dead."

CHAPTER TWENTY-NINE

It was mid-morning and sunny and, once again, I was in my favorite place, cross-legged, with Joleen next to me, hip-to-hip, her legs pulled up into a hug under her chin. We were on a small dune out in front of our rented South Beach condo. Since it was a ground level unit, we walked out our door and were at ocean's edge. "Paradise." It was like Dad's beautiful "Think Place," that huge, elegant cypress stump. This place was my "Think Place."

I kept thinking of the death of Richard Wentworth III, the unnecessary loss of human life, the pain brought to his destroyed family, but I felt relief that Joleen was no longer haunted day and night. She performed in public without fear and joined me at my events like tonight's.

"What are you thinking?"

I loved the way she could always tell when I'm thinking something through and wants to be a part of it.

"I'm rehearsing for my big speech tonight."

"Oooh."

We agreed to eliminate the nightmare of Ricky Wentworth from further discussion and from our lives together, if possible.

"I've had a complete change of heart regarding my presentation, caused, I guess, by what I see coming tonight; it's not just another Double F Group PAC effort directed at some social club. This was set to be one huge election rally, pure and simple. Double F has brought together a whole list of conservation-oriented organizations: There's Live Wildly FL, The Land Trust, Coastal Coalition, the Nature Conservancy, plus Friends of the Indian River Lagoon. They suggest it's big. There's advance publicity with signs everywhere. It's all over social media."

I tried to remember what else? I distractedly picked up a shell and tossed it at the surf.

"And there's the location: the gigantic Vero Beach High School Performing Arts Center, a max seating of 1000."

I watched Joleen nod, acknowledging crowd size. She, of course, thrived on a full house.

She responded, "So, no travelogue this time, no endangered pine forests, no golden sunsets kayaking on Lake George? No bubbling springs on the St. Johns?"

"No."

"Yeah, I think you're right."

"I'm going to let this audience have it right in the gut, no holds barred, no sparkling-clear waters."

She nodded approval.

"Am I right? This is what I plan to say, 'Here's what I stand for and what has to happen to save this state. Florida's ecology has to be job one. We're at the end of the line. The tomorrows are all gone. We are out of time. We change, or we die. I'm Clayton Ian McIver. Make me your senator.'"

"I like it."

"I just read this quote by an environmentalist. Listen to this: 'For the first time in this planet's history, one species can murder, not only the habitat, but the very population of all species.' He's talking us."

Joleen and I just looked at each other.

"Your phone, Clayt." She felt the buzz against her hip.

"What now?" I couldn't seem to leave it behind when I was on the beach. I answered it, "Hi, Dad," and put it on speaker.

"Don't be afraid to come right out and ask for their vote now!"

"OK." He never said hello first, but I got used to it.

"Knock 'em dead tonight, Boy! I know you will."

"Dad, that's some group you all put together. Wildlife protectors, clean-water folks, growth controllers. Should be a full house. Congratulations."

"Nothing to it, Son. Good luck... oh, another thing I've been wanting to talk with you about. I want you to come up, first chance, and get our sailboat, move it down there, use it, or if you don't want it, put it up for brokerage. Right there at Hinckley Brokerage in Stuart would be best."

"Dad? Wait a minute." This was not just a dad-the-cheerleader call. "You said 'our' boat. That's your boat, your pride and joy. What are you talking about?" I was shocked. No way could I even think how long that boat had been a part of him, before I was born for sure. His elegant, graceful Ocean Dancer, an old, classic, Hinckley Bermuda 40 Yawl. He moored her for years at Ponce Inlet near Daytona Beach.

"Son, my sailing days are over. And I don't have time these days. And your mother doesn't care that much about sailing anymore either."

"Now that I can't believe." She loved it. They'd taken countless weekend and moonlight trips, just the two of them.

"True, but, Son, we're getting older. I don't think we can handle her like we used to."

I'd learned everything I know about sailing from them. He absolutely worshiped it. I've heard her say, "There's nothing that can compare to being properly under sail."

"That's it, Son. I'm giving it to you. Do what you must."

That was it. The phone clicked off as usual.

We, of course, would make the trip and bring the boat home.

Joleen, who heard every word, looked at me. There was something she wanted to tell me.

"I remember a certain night, our first date…. I took you to the Ocean Grill. You were looking out over the ocean. You told me all about how he taught you sailing. Him sitting right behind you at the helm, whispering directions in your ear. How he sent you below and up into the bow to press your ear against the hull and hear the, what was it, the 'slot?' I was mesmerized by it all then, and I still am."

She paused and cocked her head.

"It could be fun, even if all we did was bring it down, and then you sold it."

"It'll be great to sail it again, even if just once, the trip down."

"You don't want to take a trip? Like the Bahamas?"

"It's fall, Joleen. We're in hurricane season."

"I hadn't thought of that. Maybe later?"

"Well," I answered, a little knowing look on my face. "There is the potential of a major storm, a hurricane, hitting coastal Florida, north or south, east or west. I'd be relieving Dad of all that. At least here, I can take steps in advance, nail it down, run and hide it, or just... run in order to run. We could run in the sailboat."

"Did you just say, run?"

"Yeah. It sure beats evacuating in a car. Look at it this way, Joleen. A hurricane has a general direction, a somewhat certain, wide, cone of direction, say westward or northwestward. Evacuating by car, which way do you run? What if the highways are all bumper-to-bumper? In Ocean Dancer, we just sail and/or power in the exact opposite direction."

"Let me think about that."

***

We stood in the pitch-black wings of the theater at 8 P.M. The big, main curtain was open, so we could glimpse the brightly lit house, which, just seconds ago, was dim. The muffled hum of hundreds of voices drifted onstage. It was a full house. I wondered if most even considered the huge population explosion, as it related to the destructive, uncontrolled building growth. What of their reaction when I must mention the paving over of the state's essential green space and destruction of our drinking water? Would they applaud at the end, when I finished speaking, and when I'm called an "unrealistic environmentalist" in the days to come? Would they elect a senator who says, "We're out of time. it's act or die?"

Footlights flooded the stage. An overhead key light beamed down on the free-standing mic, center stage. Joleen held my hand, her great "opening night" smile already spreading across her face, and we quick-stepped to center. The lights hit us.

She took the mic in hand, stepped into the key light, and said, "Hi, I'm Joleen."

A few shouts ring out. "We love you, Jo!"

Another shouted, "Sing For Us, Joleen!"

She handed the mic to me.

I wonder if they'll hear me? I stepped into the key light.

I said, "I'm Clayt McIver, and I'm asking you to make me your next senator."

I could hear a pin drop.

CHAPTER THIRTY

It was nearly noon when Joleen and I arrived at Ponce de Leon Inlet, known simply as "Ponce" by locals and area mariners.

It was a balmy fall day with small white puffy clouds scattered across the Florida blue.

I parked the rental in the lot behind the dock master's building, and we walked around to the office. Mom and Dad would pick up the car and return it for me to the rental lot in Palatka. They reported they had paid up, checked out, and moved Ocean Dancer to a nearby temporary dock at the dock master's request, and left the keys with him.

I introduced us, and he dropped the keys in my hand.

He said, "Your folks are the real thing, cruising pros. They made trip after trip back and forth with armloads of grocery bags.

Think you'll find she's ready to go with all the comforts."

As we moved outside, he went on. "Down off this main dock, second catwalk on your right, slip A2. You can see her from here, the Ocean Dancer. The Hinckley B-40, for my money, the most beautiful thing in this harbor or any other harbor."

I nodded and thanked him.

True, there's no design like the Bill Tripp Bermuda 40, built by the Henry R. Hinckley Boat Company, Southwest Harbor, Maine. She had that elegant, low slung at the hip and rising bow look, called sheer, that so defines a B-40. First one launched, I think, was about 1958.

"Can you see which one, Joleen? The sleek, glossy-white one with the tall mast forward, small mizzen mast aft." I pointed where the dock master pointed. "Look at her, shimmering white freeboard... freeboard, that's the sides up from waterline to those shiny, varnished, teak toe rails, called gunnels, all white decks, white cabin top, varnished cockpit, that's all varnished teak."

She nodded. "Looks like a string of pearls from Tiffany's."

Aboard we found the dock master's remarks absolutely true; they stocked the boat with bed linens for the main bunks and two lightweight sleeping bags in the bow cabin, a full fridge with ice, at least three breakfasts, lunches and dinners, fruit, canned goods, milk, coffee, beer, and soda. I'd first planned to get up there, take inventory, then go shopping. Mom and Dad proved once again to be the seasoned, experienced cruisers they are, just as the dock master said. I opened the little liquor cabinet in the main saloon, and there was a bottle of nice red wine and a fifth of Dewar's Scotch. That's a sailor's send-off.

I wondered how tough it was to stock the boat, then just walk away. She's such a classic, I think built mid '70's. Only two owners, the first, then Dad in the '80's. Maybe they would find time to use it again.

I hadn't been aboard for several years, except to do an occasional maintenance chore like Saturday morning rail varnishing, engine filter change, and maybe mop and hose down salt-slippery decks.

My plan was to test run the little diesel the length of the Inlet, a shakedown cruise. I'd check the filters, oil, temp, then hoist sails and check them, halyards and sheets, standing and running rigging, winches, and, of course, my crew. If happy with all, including a crew that remained enthusiastic, and the weather forecast holding, I planned to set a course out of Ponce, South by Southeast.

I wanted to clear Cape Canaveral as dawn broke tomorrow morning. I sat in the cockpit and studied both the wind speed and wind direction instrument's dials mounted on the forward bulkhead next to the companionway leading below. Since it was well into fall, nor'easters were common, some strong, some gentle.

The past few days showed a nice 7 to 10 knot breeze straight out of 35 degrees, a sailor's perfect nor'easter. The dials said it was still holding. The NOAA long-range forecast announced, holding through at least midweek.

I liked it. It was a go for me. It looked like Joleen was going to experience a 150-mile voyage on what's called a "broad reach," a heading of 150 plus or minus degrees, all sails ballooning to starboard, Ponce to home. The slot would be singing, as I hoped my crew was.

I explained the reality of the voyage to her, with no hiding the truth about conditions and dangers, stress and fatigue, the shortened sleep periods, and standing watches.

I said, "What if you're supposed to wear your harness in weather or at night on deck, and clip yourself to the rail, and you forget? Or you have your harness on but can not clip the leash to a fitting to protect you from going overboard?"

"And I fall off the boat? I know how to swim."

"How about a hundred miles? Out of sight of land?" I wondered how she'd fare. She was a smart student who listened. She was strong and knew what a long day or night was. Best of all, she wanted to learn to sail. Strangely, at least for me, I thought her new love of wind in her face has something to do with using it to its fullest in her throat. With Joleen, a dream was as real as real is, something to be perfected, or as nearly so as possible.

I checked the fuel; it was full. Dad would never forget that.

I got up to stretch my legs and was standing at the stern, mesmerized at the sparkling harbor water reflecting the afternoon sun. It was quiet all across the harbor, my mind adrift. Something bobbled in the water, several things, glistening, rolling and sparkling, likely washed into this corner by the tides. One rolled over, and the sun hit its glass tubing; the shiny glass jumped at me.

A syringe!

I jumped back. My mind shot a picture out of the past, and my memory returned it as if real. It hadn't been that long ago. My eyes climbed the trees, not wanting to look. I'd seen the distant campfire smoke curling up through the pines, inviting me to stop and, perhaps, say hello. I beached my kayak on the crushed shells along the St. Johns, stepped gingerly through high grass, passed that yellow canoe off to the side... and then, I froze. Two syringes in the arms of two young people, dead before they even started life.

Joleen saw my reaction and called, "Clayt?"

I will never forget that hideous day, that lonely night trying to sleep in the kayak after the bodies were lifted away by the sheriff's chopper. Seeing it again, now, at least carried a lesson. Honor the gift of life, all life.

My response was hesitant. I finally said, "It's nothing." I swallowed and took a deep breath. Maybe I'd tell her when we were underway.

Recovered, I said, "Let's go see how she flies."

I started the engine and gathered in the mooring lines, coiled them and, with a hitch, lashed them to the stern taffrail to dry. I dropped into the cockpit and put it in forward, all-slow. I slowly went over the checklist, one item at a time.

Up near the Inlet entrance lights, Ponce faces northeast, into this day's wind. I set the mainsail and unfurled the headsail canvas, the huge, light, genoa. I hopped back to the cockpit, eased the mainsheet way out and let the main boom fall away to starboard. I trimmed the genoa just enough to let her open full and ballooning. With not a hitch, it was a go.

I asked, "Ready?"

Joleen stepped up on deck wearing her storm harness, and said emphatically, "I m ready. I'm going forward."

Before I could even suggest that she use the guardrails and shrouds to hold onto as she went, she inched up the windward side on the port deck to stand before the mast. She snapped the harness leash shackle onto a mast eye fitting and turned smack into the wind, as I watched. She was actually singing her lyrics right into the wind. They slapped right back at her. She turned around, facing the opposite way, downwind, and her song carried away through the slot, the open tunnel of air between the two sails, and danced past me, drifting away in our wake. She stopped short, her mouth still open, totally amused at the difference.

She looked back at me and came, grabbing lifelines as she moved, and announced, "I get it! I get it! We're being pulled forward, not pushed like Cleopatra's barge!"

She was right. The air rushing through the slot, faster than the air outside the sails, caused a partial vacuum, causing us to be pulled forward. Joleen's face had a huge smile, even for her, almost childlike.

I was reminded, like a flashback, of another like face, my little Maya Muñoz, the little lost but ever so luckily found, Maya. She stood at the open passenger door of the sheriff's patrol car, turned back toward us, and smiled. Someone said, "She's smiling at you, Mr. McIver."

Joleen spoke, and my thought of little Maya faded. "Will you teach me how to put my ear against the hull and hear the slot, just like you were taught?"

I couldn't believe she remembered that from our first date at the Ocean Grill.

She said, "Tonight, will you sit close behind me with your face next to my ear and whisper directions, the way you learned?"

When I didn't respond immediately, she added, "For when, as you've said, we have to run from the inevitable hurricane."

I could only stare at the big, lit, binnacle compass on the wheel post. It read 150 degrees. The Florida Atlantic Coast runs the same, maybe 155 degrees. We would parallel it all the way home.

Deep down, in the very back of my mind, but always present, with the given of the apparently solid good weather forecast, still on my mind is … after we get home.

Beyond the speaking engagements to be arranged by the Double F Group, I had months of serious political campaigning ahead of me. Some voters may not realize the urgency we faced. They just haven't had the experiences I've had traversing the state's treasures like the St. Johns. I spent days alone and learning on that scientifically significant artery.

For example, the loss of surrounding green space to new housing. It isn't well known that green space, all open land, is the filter for turning rain into drinking water before it is stored in the aquifer, just as the rain, in turn, feeds the green space. Nor is it common knowledge that strangling of the wildlife corridor, which is green space, as well as habitat, means death to our migrating birds and animals, and, once again, loss of clean water. Not everyone visits our rivers, lakes, or estuaries. Not everyone sails, skis, swims, fishes, picnics, or sunbathes, to witness the toxic pollution that continues, or watch the deadly algae blooms spread and poison.

I must win. I must lead to stop the environmental suicide of this state on its present course. Nature has made it quite clear, you take away Florida's natural resources, you pave over her green space, Mother Nature will take away your water. It's all connected. Loss of water will take away the possibility of Man existing here.

The late afternoon was giving way to an auburn twilight, the light breeze steady. All sails were full and quietly pulling us. My fingers on the helm, I sat back for the long reach ahead. The sailing was silent, except for our own gentle wake. I thought I heard a vaguely familiar sound I once heard when lost, alone and so lonely on the St. Johns, a song, clear and throaty, hollow and distant. I thought then it might be a bird calling her mate or simply something carried on a sound wave.

She sang again for me.

We kissed.

We set our course.

ABOUT THE AUTHOR

Growing up on the Great Lakes, he was an expert sailor, held a U. S. Coast Guard Power/Sail Ocean Master license, and owned a sailboat, Pendancing.

In 1970, Pete Clements moved to Vero Beach, Florida and founded a marine business while he continued to write newspaper columns and magazine articles.

By the mid-1990s, he was a full-time novelist. His debut novel, *The Latitude*, was Honoree Finalist in the 2020 Eric Hoffer International Awards. Recently, the novel won the 2023 IndieReader Discovery Award and the Literary Titan Award.

Pete continues to live in Vero Beach and his new novel, *The Last Floridian*, will be released December 2023.

Pete Clements is a lifetime writer and former member of the Directors Guild of America.

LITERARY TITAN
BOOK AWARD
FINALIST
First Horizon Award
The Eric Hoffer Book Award
THE
LATITUDE
INDIE READER
WINNER
DISCOVERY AWARDS
Pete Clements

NOTE FROM PETE CLEMENTS

Word-of-mouth is crucial for any author to succeed. If you enjoyed *The Last Floridian*, please leave a review online—anywhere you are able. Even if it's just a sentence or two. It would make all the difference and would be very much appreciated.

Thanks!
Pete Clements

We hope you enjoyed reading this title from:

www.blackrosewriting.com

Subscribe to our mailing list – *The Rosevine* – and receive
FREE books, daily deals, and stay current with news about
upcoming releases and our hottest authors.
Scan the QR code below to sign up.

Already a subscriber? Please accept a sincere thank you for
being a fan of Black Rose Writing authors.

View other Black Rose Writing titles at
www.blackrosewriting.com/books and use promo
code
PRINT to receive a **20% discount** when purchasing.